COME WEST AND SEE

COME

 W. W. NORTON & COMPANY

Independent Publishers Since 1923

New York | London

WEST AND SEE

stories

MAXIM LOSKUTOFF

Copyright © 2018 by Maxim Loskutoff

All rights reserved
Printed in the United States of America
First Edition

For information about permission to reproduce selections from this book, write to Permissions, W. W. Norton & Company, Inc., 500 Fifth Avenue, New York, NY 10110

For information about special discounts for bulk purchases, please contact W. W. Norton Special Sales at specialsales@wwnorton.com or 800-233-4830

Manufacturing by Quad Graphics, Fairfield
Book design by Chris Welch
Production manager: Lauren Abbate

Library of Congress Cataloging-in-Publication Data

Names: Loskutoff, Maxim, author.
Title: Come west and see: stories / Maxim Loskutoff.
Description: First edition. | New York: W. W. Norton & Company, 2018.
Identifiers: LCCN 2017059973 | ISBN 9780393635584 (hardcover)
Classification: LCC PS3612.O7733 A6 2018 | DDC 813/.6—dc23
LC record available at https://lccn.loc.gov/2017059973

W. W. Norton & Company, Inc., 500 Fifth Avenue, New York, N.Y. 10110
www.wwnorton.com

W. W. Norton & Company Ltd., 15 Carlisle Street, London W1D 3BS

1 2 3 4 5 6 7 8 9 0

For Mom and Dad

Who knows what the future holds
Or where the cards may fall
But if you don't come out West and see
You'll never know at all.

—LUCINDA WILLIAMS

CONTENTS

MONTANA TERRITORY,
1893

THE DANCING BEAR

FIRST, SHE WAS THE SOUND OF A BREAKING BRANCH. A SPLIN-tered knucklecrack shattering the quiet of these western Montana woods. It is a heavy quiet here, and no good comes when it is broken. Red men, gunslingers, and all manner of gold-crazy down-and-outs plague this wild country. My heart went to scampering.

I took up my Winchester and crept to the door. Early light played on the mud-daubed timber walls. I built this cabin ten years ago with naught but a hatchet, five yards of rope, and Ezekiel—a mule by then more dead than alive. Damned if I would give it up without a fight.

Another branch snapped and I toed the door open. The

smell of dew-wet pine wafted in. I slid the rifle's nose into the crack. I held my breath.

She was up on her haunches, weight back—all six hundred pounds of it, her arms raised, like the dancing bear I saw in Barnum & Bailey's Fantastic Roadshow when I was a boy. But this was no dancing bear. She was a grizzly. Eight feet tall and used to having her way in the world. Her dinner-plate paws thrashed apples from my apple tree. She huffed and snorted, blowing clouds of steam. She was gorging on fruit, preparing for hibernation, and I believe she was enjoying herself. The rising sun smoldered the crest of Scapegoat Ridge above her massive head.

I thought to shoot her. Even leveled the Winchester's barrel. Her pelt would have fetched a hefty price. But I could not pull the trigger. She was magnificent. All the dreadful beauty of this territory was bound up in her figure. She ate the apples whole, holding them up between her paws and crushing them with her molars. Her fur shimmered and rolled in waves, like the windy prairie where I was born. Her pink tongue swept stray apple chunks from around her mouth.

I wondered if she had lips.

She stood to her full height, reaching for an apple high in the branches. Her body was shapely: trunk thighs widening into hips, slimming a bit through her middle before expanding again into the muscled bulk of her shoulders. She jumped and swung and caught the apple on her first claw—her index claw—and, with a snarl, tore it from the branch.

I had planned to save the apples and enjoy them as a treat

on cold winter nights (nights when my cabin is a lump in the snow), but I was not angry at the bear. I was happy to watch her. I wondered if there were breasts beneath her fur.

I suddenly realized I was erect. Confusion and shame roiled my gut. I had never thought to lie with a bear before, but once I began I could not stop. I knelt, hiding my swollen cock behind the doorjamb, and, instead of thinking of protecting my home, I imagined running into her great hairy arms. Licking her throat. Inhaling her smell. Finding her tongue with mine, tasting apples. Tumbling back into the grass, her legs clamped around my buttocks, both of us sticky with apple juice. Warmth. Brown eyes. A roaring tangle of limbs.

I was dizzy, the rifle slack in my arms. She looked at me, wiped her jaws, and ambled back into the woods as the sun rose over Rattlesnake Canyon.

SHE CAME BACK the next morning, and the next. I took to waiting for her, first in my long johns and then naked. I stood in the doorway letting the morning sun draw the chill from my skin. She would watch me, sometimes for several minutes, unconcerned, before returning to the apples. I squared my shoulders and stuck out my chest.

My days fell into a friendly pattern. There is a deep pool in a bend of Rattlesnake Creek just east of my cabin. It is fed by melted snow from the Mission Mountains. After the bear made her way back into the forest, I would run, still naked, and plunge into the icy water. I slid around the rocky streambed like a trout. I emerged dripping, every inch of my body a-tingle, feeling younger than I had in years. Then I would wrap myself in a blanket and make coffee over the stove.

I spent the afternoons hiking through the woods checking my traps, killing and skinning what I caught. Boulders fill a ravine cutting down from the highest point on Scapegoat Ridge. Each day I carried one as far as I could, hoping to impress the bear with my strength. I stopped cutting my nails. When they were long enough, I sharpened the ends. I had the notion that, if we were to make love, she would want to feel my claws in her back.

I treated myself to a cup of whiskey in the evenings. I sat by the creek with my back against a birch as the first stars showed themselves. I sipped the whiskey and whittled toys for the furry, indistinct children that wandered around the edges of my mind.

I do not know if the bear noticed my expanding muscles, but she became comfortable with me and continued to visit even after the apples were gone and the nip of fall was replaced by November's true chill. She would sit in the clearing surrounded by lodgepole pines, snuffling at the morning air and running her claws through the fur on her belly as I shivered in the doorway. She was quite fat by then. I knew the day would soon come when she took cover for her winter sleep.

I dreaded it.

I was never brave enough to step out of my doorway. I stood there, throwing off sparks, wanting desperately to go to her, but paralyzed. I have lingered many times atop high cliffs, tempted to step into the abyss. It was this same feeling with the bear. She could easily tear me limb from limb, rake her claws down my spine, and eat me—bones and all. Part of me wanted her to. I had been alone for a long time.

I BEGAN TO FEAR for my sanity a month after the bear went into hibernation. The first true snow had fallen the night before, and as the wind whipped through the windows, rattling my pans and keeping me from sleep, I did a shameful thing.

I was heartsick. I had grown used to a dull emptiness—such is the life of a trapper in the Montana and Oregon Territories—but this new feeling was sharp. Desperate. I wanted nothing more than to find the cave where she slept, curl up in her arms, and so, too, dream the winter away.

I had made a fine haul that day. The beaver and muskrat, sensing the deeper snows to come, were anxious for food—vulnerable. Fifteen fresh pelts were strung above my doorway. Their rich animal smell reminded me of the bear. I took them down and arranged them on the floor in a bear shape: legs, arms, head . . . Then I stripped and lay flat on my stomach on the skins. I thought of her: the muscles in her rump, the way she snorted with pleasure over a ripe apple. I opened my mouth and sucked on the fur. I licked it. I wriggled my hips, moaning. The cold wind slapped my back.

Seeing the sticky furry mess on the floor the next morning, I was filled with dread. Years before, hiking through dense cedar forest on the Kitsap Peninsula, I came across the body of a fellow trapper. His corpse was sprawled over a knobby root. Before shooting himself, he had used his skinning knife to carve the word *meat* into his own skin. *Meat* in jagged letters on his chest, his thighs, even his neck. Scavengers had eaten his nose and eyes, but I could still tell he was a young man. I covered him with dirt. His eyeless face visits me when I feel my own mind slipping into the darkened woods.

I decided to go into Missoula at once to lie with a woman at the Golden Rose.

THE HIKE INTO MISSOULA is twenty-two miles along unmapped game trails. I filled my pack with dried venison and hardtack and set out with my longest knife. I hacked away the thimbleberry bushes that had grown across the path since my last trip into town. A fine layer of snow covered their thin branches. Deer and rodent tracks spotted the ground. I caught myself searching for the bear's familiar paw. I shook my head and hurried on.

I arrived just before dark, tired in body but not in mind. Missoula is a fast-changing place. I remember when it was nothing more than several saloons and a general store stubbornly gathered on a bend of the Clark Fork River. Now they are building a university. The foundations surround a grassy oval at the foot of Mount Sentinel. I have to laugh to think of such learned folk in a town where it is often joked that a man's life is worth less than his boots.

The Golden Rose is a timber-frame building with a peaked roof and red tassels hanging limply from the eaves. The once-bright red paint on the trim has flaked away and taken on the quality of dried blood. It faces Higgins Avenue, beside Holcombe's Curiosities, but the entrance is in the alley around back. I knocked the dirt from my boots on the red doorframe and stepped inside.

I stood dumbly in the parlor staring up at a large oil painting of General Custer ravaging a Sioux camp. His yellow beard was flecked with blood. I wondered what else new I would find inside. If the whores spoke Latin now, or oiled their hair straight up from their heads. A chandelier warmed the room with gold light. Chrystal decanters holding all manner of spirits lined the shelves above the bar. There was no one behind it. I smelled strawberry perfume and my own mountain stink.

Bad Lucy padded through a bead curtain, smoothing the front of her black dress. She was a beauty once, the kind you paid extra for, but age had sunk her cheeks. "Bill," she said. "It's been years."

I nodded. The translucent skin on her arms revealed ropy purple veins.

"You'll be needing a bath."

She led me upstairs past framed pictures of girls in dark garters tiredly eyeing the camera, and one of a mountain lion roaring and reared back on its hind legs, to a small room with a claw-foot tub. I peered down her dress as she twisted the faucet knobs. Her shrunk wrinkled breasts hung like testicles.

Even so, I was heartened by a stirring in my loins. Steam thickened the air.

"These will have to be cut as well." She gestured at my claws.

She left the room and I undressed, carefully folding my dirt-stiff garments. I felt savage and oversized as I lowered my body into the small tub. I caught sight of my reflection in the teardrop mirror on the far wall and my heart fell. My body had taken on the stringy, leathery quality of a thing left too long in the sun. My beard was matted into a single clump and stuck to my chest. Mucus crusted my nostrils. Wiry tufts sprang from my eyebrows. I looked every bit the mad woodsman, and I knew that whatever girl I chose would be disappointed.

The hot water loosened my muscles. I sank beneath it, blowing bubbles to the surface. I was a regular at the Golden Rose when I first settled in Rattlesnake Canyon ten years ago. There was a whore named Molly I took to hard. She was red Irish. Mean. A scratcher. She loved to laugh at the sad types who washed up in such territorial outposts. I deluded myself into believing that she joked with me in confidence—that I was special to her because she told me how Jack Kipp's wife had left him for an Indian, or that Doc Evaro, who owned the general store, liked a finger in his anus.

When my cabin was finished, I asked her to come live with me. I told her about the clearing on the creek and how the shadows of the lodgepole pines were like friends in the evening. I told her about the apple tree I had planted and that she could have a garden. She did not laugh in my face, but I could tell she would laugh as soon as I left, and many more times when she told the story.

My hankerings faded after that. I figured I was past the age of passion, and decided there must be something better for a man to spend his money on than women. I bought a set of books—Greek epics—from a schoolteacher returning east, and took some comfort reading them aloud. I would march along Scapegoat Ridge pretending to be Odysseus lost at the western edge of the world.

Now I was back, and I worried that coming had been a mistake. I finished my bath and set to work on my nails. They were thick and hard and the clippers Bad Lucy had left were dull. I clipped and clipped hopelessly. Trimmed nails or no, I was an ugly man who belonged in the woods, where no one could see me but the animals.

I PAID BAD LUCY a large sum (they claim that statehood and modern advancements lead to lower prices, but my experience has been just the opposite) and her smile sweetened. She whistled for the girls. They formed a line in front of the bar. Their painted faces seemed to be made entirely of slashes and bone. One of them lit a cigar from the sputtering oil lamp. She bit down on the end and her face was lost in smoke. Another had a black-haired baby dripping from her breast. I grinned at them. They looked through me to the opposite wall. The grin stuck fast to my face.

I selected the girl with the longest hair. Light brown, it fell past her waist. I followed her upstairs, and she told me her name was Frances, like the First Lady. She brought me to the third of eight rooms on the second floor. There was a cot, a mirror, and a small table covered in bottled creams, each of which cost extra. I closed the door and Frances sat down on the edge of the bed. She looked out the small window at the dusk-lit rooftops. Workers sat along the eaves of the mercantile, a second story going up behind them.

I struggled with the many silk ribbons securing her scarlet bodice. My fingers shook, unused to such delicate work. I kept my eyes on her hair. I thought of the warmth inside my cabin on spring mornings, the cold clearness of the stream, and the way the bear raised her head in the brilliant flood of sunlight over Scapegoat Ridge. Finally, I finished and Frances shrugged her shoulders. The bodice fell to the floor and her flesh settled into a roll at her waist. She sighed. A whip scar divided her pale back from shoulder to hip. All manner of tragedies must have led her to this room, and men like me. Her skin smelled oversweet, like spoiled fruit. A queasy desperation, either to run, or cry, or throw her to the ground, rose in my throat. I licked her neck. She inhaled sharply. I squeezed her breasts. I bit them. I tried not to think about the bear.

She pinched my ear in warning. "No marks," she said. Then she lay back and spread her legs. A tiny tuft of hair, much smaller than my fist, rose between her pale thighs. Everywhere else on her body was utterly bare. I stared, horrified.

I rushed from the room, clattered down the stairs, and

pushed through the bead curtain. Bad Lucy was at her desk writing in a leather-bound book.

"She's but a child!" I sputtered. I was fairly shaking. I had heard of houses in Virginia City where such things could be had for a price, but I did not think Bad Lucy would sink so low. Even with so many changes, I could not believe such foulness had become commonplace.

She swiveled to face me. "I can assure you, she's nineteen and seven months."

I shook my head, motioning at my groin in an attempt to convey hairlessness.

Bad Lucy narrowed her eyes. "Did you expect a forest?"

My face reddened. I thought of how I'd run from the room, leaving Frances on the bed. I tried to picture my big hairy body atop her small hairless one. "I want a different girl. Older."

"Do as you like," Bad Lucy said, her face stone, "but you've paid for this one. If you want another, you'll pay again."

I began to argue and a large man appeared in the doorway. He wore a floral vest and held a tomahawk in his right hand. I could tell by his face that it would not mean much to him to shed my blood. I bowed my head and edged past him.

"You're a fool, Bill," Bad Lucy called after me.

THE REST OF THE WINTER was cold and dark and I would be a liar if I did not admit that on several occasions I arranged pelts on the floor and lay down upon them.

THE BEAR CAME BACK in March and what I had known in my heart was proven as fact: she was a she, for she had a cub. It was three feet tall and nearly as wide. The beaked sedge at the edge of the clearing tickled its nose. Its coat was ashy brown with a white marking around the throat. It romped around its mother's feet as she approached the apple tree. She was thin. Disturbingly so. Her skin hung loose and I could see her collarbone against her fur. The little creature had been sucking her dry.

She sat beneath the tree. Small leaves and buds sprouted from the branches. She nipped off one of the buds and chewed it thoughtfully. The cub batted her knees. I saw worry in her brown eyes. She shooed the cub away and it circled her and jumped on her back. I covered my genitals with a pot.

The sky was gray and swollen, about to rain.

She ate two more buds, then wedged her back against the trunk and writhed up and down on the rough bark. Her long winter coat was falling out. She growled with pleasure. It would have been perfect—especially after so long—were it not for the cub. It sat beside a stump. It ate a piece of grass. A red-tailed hawk flew overhead and it jumped away from the shadow, then it jumped away from the first raindrops. The pot was cold on my thighs.

A butterfly flitted up from the creek and the cub galloped after it, snapping. It crashed through a chokecherry bush and disappeared into the forest. The mother followed. My clearing was empty again. Wisps of her hair clung to the abandoned trunk.

It had been an idyllic scene but it left my heart so heavy I could not carry it around for the rest of the day. There are thirty-six knots in the Douglas fir planks that make up my ceiling. I lay in bed and counted them over and over as the rain drummed the roof.

I only left the cabin to put a strip of venison in the branches of the apple tree. She was so thin.

THE SIX DAYS that followed were all much the same. I left meat for her in the tree each night—high in the branches where the coyotes and wolves could not reach. Then I rested against the trunk. I imagined I could still feel her warmth. I filled my pockets with her hair, thinking I might make a pillow or undergarment.

The mountains around me seemed to grow as the sun set.

I hardly slept. I rolled from one side of my straw mattress to the other. Several times each night, I would get up, pour myself a cup of whiskey, and sit on the edge of my bed. The ghostly birches swaying outside my window were like skeletons holding hands. I curled my toes on the cold dirt floor. My few belongings were pieces of shadow. I thought back on my solitary life, following game from one forest to the next, always a step ahead of civilization. It had not amounted to much.

I tried to shake my melancholy with more whiskey. I told

a knot in the ceiling about all the wonders I had seen, all the beasts I had shot. My adventures in country that is, I suspect, the most beautiful in the world. But I could not escape the feeling that much of my life had slipped away, and now the bear was slipping away, too.

She came back each morning but it was not the same. After taking the meat from the tree, she would sit and watch her cub play. It liked to dive headfirst into the dirt and roll over in a somersault. It looked up at the sky, stunned, each time this maneuver was completed successfully. Then it would run to her and she would lick away the burs and nettles that clung to its fur.

I imagined the feel of her tongue.

ON THE SEVENTH DAY, I woke with a determination I had not known in years, perhaps since the day I resolved never to see Molly nor any other woman again.

It was an unseasonably warm spring morning. Pale green shoots pushed through the earth. Arrowleaf flowers splashed yellow on the face of Scapegoat Hill. The creek was full and loud.

The bears came as the first rays of sunlight lit gold the tree-tops and sent insects buzzing up through shafts of light. She made straight for the apple tree. She stood on her hind legs, showing off her fine shape, and plucked the meat from where I'd wedged it in the branches. She was regaining her weight.

The cub sniffed around the edge of the clearing. It tripped on a rock. It was a round, clumsy, stupid thing.

I picked up the Winchester from beside the door and steadied it against my shoulder. The familiar weight comforted me. A single purple flower hung from the cub's coat. It paused and looked up at a mockingbird winging south. I aimed first at its mother, reminding myself of the fine price her pelt would fetch, the books and other comforts I could buy. Her winter coat was gone and her fur shimmered, golden, like the morning we met. She was so beautiful. I swung the barrel down to the foolish little creature who was taking her from me.

Without thinking, I pulled the trigger.

The shot shattered the morning. The cub was knocked backward, twisting. Its legs flew into the air. It went hard to the dirt on its back, raising a puff of dust. Four small paws treaded the air, and then went still. The purple flower drifted lazily down beside it.

I turned back to the mother. She was frozen, staring at her fallen cub. Her eyes moved wildly around the clearing, back to her cub, and again around the clearing. A cracked bellowing noise came from deep in her gut. She reared up to her full height and bellowed again. She did not notice me in the doorway, where I always was.

I threw aside the rifle and ran toward her, plunging through the grass, mad with grief and shame. I leapt over a stump. I reached out for her. She dropped down, turned, and ran on all fours into the woods.

———

SUMMER TURNED TO FALL. Crows peck at the meat I leave for her in the branches. They cackle amid the garlands of rotting deer flesh and the ripe red apples.

I wrap the cub's pelt around my shoulders. I slide its head over my head and hunch down. The rich smell fills my nose. I put my hands on its paws and crawl to the tree.

I wait for her to come back for me.

COME WEST AND SEE

END TIMES

I

ELLI WOULDN'T LET ME STOP UNTIL WE'D CROSSED THE LINE
into Utah. She was a nail in the passenger seat—rigid, sharp,
her blue eyes darting back and forth between the speedometer
and the double yellow lines. Dry rivers of makeup connected
her eyes to her chin. Leon lay where I'd put him across the
backseat. His chin was propped on a pile of Carlos Castaneda
paperbacks. Strands of drool hung from the orange spines.
His haunches trembled whenever we went over a bump. His
glazed, suffering face was fixed on the back of Elli's bare shoulder. We'd gotten most of the blood out of the slate-colored fur
on his back but there were still flecks on his pale belly.

Route 89 flanked the scrub brush and dust of Arizona
for thirty miles before turning north through Kanab. A

half-empty bottle of Popov rattled in the cupholder. Elli lifted it by the neck. "We might need that," I said. She paused, considering, and then sipped it anyway. Power lines, suspended from transformer towers, were strung across the sky as far as I could see. Probably they ran all the way down to Mexico, like bandits.

Kanab only had one gas station, a neat little Sinclair with a scrubbed forecourt and gleaming green pumps. I pulled in, parked. It hardly even smelled like gas, the air was so fresh. A pine forest came right up behind the store. HOME OF THE STATE CHAMPION LADY RAMS read a banner on the window where the beer advertisements should've been. I put my foot on the concrete plinth beneath the pump, swiped my credit card, and lifted the nozzle from its holster.

Elli got out and stretched. Her long torso gave her a snaky, undulating look as she leaned right and left, her arms over her head, her bare feet on the pavement. She walked stiffly to the bathroom at the side of the store, rolling her neck. *Put some shoes on*, I wanted to yell after her, but I knew she wouldn't. She was free-spirited about germs, money, underwear, and directions. Everything else she worried about.

A clump of fur clung to the hem of her orange dress. One of the shoulder straps had fallen. It hovered above her elbow. Clothes had a way of slipping off her frame, unable to disguise the girl beneath. My shoulders ached from driving all day, and from carrying Leon.

She came out with a wad of wet paper towels, her face radiant with worry. She opened the Sentra's dust-sprayed back

door and started dabbing the fur around Leon's wound. We'd
doused it in vodka and bandaged it up as best we could with
athletic tape and a clean T-shirt from my gym bag. The bullet
had gone in through his hip. I wondered if it was a bad place
for a coyote to get shot—if they kept any organs back there.

"He'll be fixed up by this time tomorrow," I said. "He'll
make it."

Elli didn't answer. She just kept dabbing. Her thin arms
were surprisingly muscular. She didn't work out, but she was
tense all the time. Even in sleep she ground her teeth. Leon
didn't complain about her touching him. He never did; never
growled, not so much as a snort. Elli put her cracked lips
against his nose. Their eyes met.

A gust of wind came in from the north and I shivered as I
replaced the nozzle. We were climbing into winter latitudes.
"Montana," she'd said, when I emerged from the canyon with
Leon a bleeding bundle in my arms, the first time he'd let me
carry him since he was a pup. She knew a vet there, a friend of
her father's. She'd seen him bring a shot wolf back from worse,
apparently, and he wouldn't report us to Animal Control.

"Everything okay?" the cashier asked, when I went in to
buy some water and ChapStick. She was prettier than most
women who work in gas stations. Tan, with feather earrings
and a mother's worried smile.

I nodded, realizing there was blood dried on my shirt.
"Spilled some coffee."

Mountains began to break through the desert. Red ones
first: mesas, buttes, hoodoos. I told Elli about the time my

father took us to Zion. We stayed in a Travelodge in Hurricane. It had HBO, and my brother and I just wanted to stay in the room and watch. My dad got so angry that he broke the TV screen with his fist and we went home two days early. Elli traced triangles on the window with her finger as the yellow-brown landscape blurred by. She wasn't listening. Her lips, wet now with ChapStick, were pressed together. Freckles shone through the makeup carelessly dusted on her nose. She was beautiful in a wrung-out, haggard sort of way that I couldn't get over, even after three years.

Leon peed. It hissed onto the floor, soaking the carpet and empty Styrofoam cups under my seat. The sweet toxic vinegar stink made my eyes water.

Elli turned and watched him struggling to get out of his mess. He knocked two of the books off the seat. His paw flailed the air. His hind leg was soaked, the wet fur matted to the bone. Yellow drops slid down the plastic seat cover onto the floor. "It's okay," she said. "It's okay."

I rolled the windows down and let the dry air blast my face. We merged onto I-15: four wide lanes running north all the way to Butte. I kept my eyes away from the rearview mirror. In a day or two, three at most, I'd be back home, freshly showered, lying on my couch with a cold beer, watching women's tennis. Brown grass grew through gravel in the median. Semis rattled as we passed, spitting diesel from their dark underbellies.

An hour went by before Elli spoke. "He needs food," she said.

"It'll just make him shit," I answered.

She looked at me like I was a half-squashed insect.

"I'm kidding," I said. "C'mon."

I took the Nephi exit and drove up and down the quiet Mormon streets, past rows of white clapboard houses with blue trim and lawns mowed down to a military stubble. There was a gun store, a confectioner's, a sign that read YOU ARE NOT ALONE. I didn't know what we were looking for. Leon liked to eat cats, and he liked to eat them when they were still alive. I suggested using catnip as chum to lure one into the car.

"It isn't funny," Elli said.

We found a shaded parking spot behind the Country Kitchen, between a dumpster and a waxed red Mustang, probably the manager's—some kind of hotshot. I changed shirts, gathered the piss-soaked cups in the old one, and threw the whole mess into the dumpster. Elli cracked the windows. She opened the back door and promised Leon we'd be back soon. I came and stood beside her. Her head barely crested my shoulder. If she ever left, the fresh coral scent of her scalp would haunt me. "Be good," she said, like he was her own son. "Stay."

He lifted his head off the books and blinked. His amber eyes were wider than usual, glowing in the short white hair around them. His mouth was clamped shut. He was embarrassed, hurting. When he was happy, his mouth lolled open in a toothy grin. I reached out to touch his face. He whipped his jaws at my fingers, snapping.

"Goddammit." I jerked my hand away. He'd bitten me once,

and I still had two small scars beneath my thumb. He was five times that size now. His incisors were a half-inch long and I'd seen what they could do to a cat's skull. My ears rang. I wanted to hit him. I turned and walked quickly toward the restaurant.

Elli murmured to him, gently shut the door, and followed me inside.

The waitress led us to a booth in the corner. Each of her thighs was as wide as Elli. Her blue apron was stretched tight across her groin like a linebacker's jockstrap. I hoped the Mustang was hers. The vinyl covering the booth squeaked when I sat down. There were paper place mats and a cup of crayons. Elli looked out the window at a gray steeple knifing into the sky. Her bleached hair was cut one length all around, at her chin. We'd been out all night searching for Leon. Neither of us had slept. Her face was drawn and gray at the edges, marked by exhaustion, physically beat, but also lit by it, as if she were becoming more alive.

She ordered a cherry malt and a steak.

"You need food, too," I said.

"I'll eat the potatoes."

The steeple didn't have a crucifix but it was a church, sure enough. I'd heard somewhere that you had to be a Mormon to go into a Mormon church. I wondered if that was true, and, if so, what was inside. I drew a bandit in green on my place mat—masked and running, gun smoke far behind.

The waitress brought the malt on a silver tray. A cloud of whipped cream floated on top. Elli gave it all of her attention. The tendons in her neck stretched tight as she worked the straw. The skin on her right shoulder was sunburned red from the car window.

"Slow down," I said. "Your brain will freeze."

When the glass was empty, Elli folded the straw into a triangle. She filled the triangle with salt—a white pyramid. Dry blood was crusted around her nails.

"He tried to bite me," I said.

She broke a grain of salt with her thumbnail. "He's hurt and scared."

"Well, they'd kill him here. All these hunters." I nodded at the empty street.

Country music was playing softly and the waitress snapped her fingers just once as she pushed through the swinging doors into the kitchen. My burger came out separated into components on the plate: lettuce, tomato, onion, bun—all lined up next to the patty. Elli watched me put it together and then she watched me eat. The steak in front of her was shaped like Nevada and just as barren. I could tell she was counting the seconds in her head—*tick, tick, tick*. The waitress was leaning on the counter by the pies, watching me, too. I hardly chewed.

When the check came, Elli didn't ask for a box. She just wrapped the steak in a napkin and carried it out, dripping, in her bare hand. I left a big tip and followed her, smiling apologetically.

The air outside was sharp with the coppery smell of exhaust. Goose bumps rose on her bare arms. A drop of steak juice ran down her calf. It had been hot in Phoenix when we left. Now dusk was settling over the Wasatch Mountains. The snowy ridges made a jagged pink EKG running north. I put my hand on her shoulder, feeling the bones beneath the sunburned warmth.

"It was Rod," she said, opening the back door. "I know it was."

I shook my head. "There's lots of people it could have been."

"It was Rod." She held the steak out to Leon. I told her to be careful, but it wasn't necessary. He ate it gently, keeping his teeth away from her fingers. He nodded his head back after each bite, gulping down the meat. Juice clung to his whiskers. He glanced at me smugly.

"Rod's a fag," I said. "They don't have guns."

Leon finished and licked Elli's hands clean. "They have cats."

"Had." I laughed, despite myself.

Elli exhaled, long and slow, and I pictured myself as a chart inside her head. Two sides: good and bad, with scraps of conversation, things I'd done, memories, posted on either side. The bad side just kept filling up.

"I'm doing this for you, you know," I said. "Skipping work, driving all this way. I mean, I care about Leon."

"Do you?" she asked.

"Of course." Anger warmed my chest. "But he's a wild animal."

She squeezed his skull, massaging the base of his ears. "So you'd let him die?"

"You know that's not what I meant." But maybe it was. He'd

been trouble since the day we found him two years before, abandoned and starving by Tortilla Flat Road. Probably his mother got shot, too. For some people that was a reasonable response to a coyote. He stank up our bed, gnawed the baseboard, shed everywhere. I'd find cat parts strewn around the yard: a paw wedged in the gate, innards on the tomato plants, a half-chewed skull on the welcome mat. He'd start to growl whenever I raised my voice at Elli.

He pressed his long bristly chin into her hands and licked her wrist. "We're almost there, love," she whispered. "Just a few more hours."

I turned the heat on and we continued north. I held the needle at seventy-five for a while—I didn't know what I'd say if a cop pulled us over—but Elli kept staring at me, so I edged it up over eighty. The big empty plains closed around us. The only light was the wedge of the high beams. I was exhausted. My head hurt. The muscles in my thighs ached from climbing up and down the canyon walls, tripping in the dark. Leon had been well hidden in a dugout between two boulders. I'd found him and carried him out. Elli seemed to have forgotten that.

She sat with her feet up on the passenger seat, her arms wrapped around her shins, her thighs against her stomach. Her chin hovered above her knees. The dashboard lights shone hazy and green on her drawn face. Her left eye twitched, the pinched skin revealing the pattern of future wrinkles. The man on the radio spoke of violence from the edges of the Redoubt, armed protesters taking over a wildlife refuge. We listened until it crackled and turned to static. What was happening out there in the dark? I knew there were farmhouses and pastures not far off but it felt like the world could end and we wouldn't know till morning.

Trying to stay awake, I pictured Elli naked. Right there in the passenger seat, like she was, except the dress gone. Her thin muscled arms wrapped around her knees. The skin over her ribs scratched and bruised from clambering through the canyon. Her body folded over itself, pressed together, the color of wheat.

I put my hand on her knee. I let it slide down the smooth ladder of scars to where I could feel the rough lace hem of her underwear. She shifted away from me, pushing down my hand and her dress.

Fine, I thought. Fine fine fine.

Salt Lake City was a ghost beneath the freeway: silent buildings forming the uneven steps of a skyline at night, the slow blink of airport lights. The temple, with its turrets and balustrade, looked like a lost castle stranded on the wrong continent. An American flag hung motionless on a hilltop, lit from below.

Past the city limits, the houses gave way to fields lined with huge crouching sprinklers. One of them was on, throwing arcs of mist into the night. Time sped up and skipped forward. I thought of my father hosing blood from the bed of his truck when I was a boy, a buck splayed awkwardly across the workbench in the open garage. How long I'd knelt beside it, hoping it would stir. The car was so warm. My head fell, then jerked upright.

"We have to stop," I said. "Get some rest."

"I'll drive."

We switched places at another gas station. The clerk watched us through the window, a toothpick rolling between his lips. He was black. Black in Utah. It couldn't be easy. The motel next door was a long low twenty-roomer slung around a parking lot. THUNDERBIRD read the blue neon sign. I knew the mattresses were probably thin with stained yellow sheets and sharp springs, but I didn't care. I just wanted to stretch out. Leon's eyes gleamed in the rearview mirror. Part of his tongue hung between his teeth, pink as bubble gum.

Elli drove with both hands on the wheel, ten and two. Her lips moved every once in a while. Pursing into an almost kiss, then pulling back over her teeth.

"Does this vet have beds?" I asked.

"At his trailer," she said. "Go to sleep. I'll wake you."

I let my head roll against the seat. It smelled like fur and piss. The engine hummed beneath me and I imagined giant horses and giant natives, a hundred feet tall, thundering over the dark mountains.

The car was stopped when I awoke. We were on the shoulder, a vast plain all around. The headlights were off. Pure black, and above, a field of stars. I blinked, trying to swallow some moisture into my parched mouth. "Look," Elli whispered.

Leon was sitting up. His front paws were propped unsteadily on the shifting covers of the books. His nose was pushed against the window. His scrawny body—only two, still a puppy—was angled down to where his wounded hind-quarters rested on the seat. His eyes were fixed on the waning thumbnail of moon, as if it held the answer to all suffering.

The dark southern hills rose and fell like waves. His breath fogged the glass.

He pressed his long gray ears flat against his skull, opened his mouth, and howled. High and sharp, the sound sliced open the roof and carried into the night. He held the note. Piercing. Desperate. It was so loud it hurt my eardrums.

Elli was twisted around in the driver's seat, stretched toward him, her face contorted—love and fear and awe—her skin the same color as the moon.

"No!" I said. "No barking."

His haunches shook. He slipped and fell against the door. Elli turned and stared at me. Her bared eyes held something frightening: disgust, maybe, or the beginning of hatred. "Get out," she said.

I looked at her blankly. A few strands of her hair stuck to the headrest, straight out beside her, taut with static electricity. I had no idea where we were. Leon was chewing apart my life.

"Please. Just give us a minute alone."

I fumbled with the door; I kept yanking the handle until she reached across my chest and unlocked it. I pushed it open. The cold night air stung my face. I stood up, dazed, then leaned back into the car. Leon scrabbled on the plastic seat cover in the back. Elli watched me, the disgust in her eyes mixing with a pity I couldn't bear, as if I were the wounded creature helpless in the night.

"He's going to die," I said, and slammed the door.

Pebbles crunched beneath my sneakers. I walked away from the highway, down into a ditch, and back up again. I smelled snow, trees. Idaho, maybe. Orion's belt and the Big Dipper hung at opposite ends of the sky. I couldn't remember any of the other constellations. Just a mess of stars.

II

I lay on my back on the air mattress in the sagging screen porch behind Hutch's trailer, smelling mold and fur and the ponderosa pines that blackly pierced the dawn. The mattress hissed softly, deflating beneath my weight. All the wounded animals on the decrepit compound were beginning to awaken: dogs barked, parrots squawked from the aviary, big cats rustled in the long cage-lined Quonset hut. I lay very still, gripped by a nameless anxiety. Leon was still alive, but something else, I was afraid, was not.

Ashen light slanted through cracks in the slat roof. My clothes felt like I'd been wearing them for much longer than a day. I thought to shower but didn't move.

Elli came in from the operating room. She paused in the doorway. Her expression was distant, lost. I wanted her to come and lie down exactly on top of me, the length of her body against mine, nose to nose, lips to lips, our breath one continuous stream. Then maybe I would sleep.

Instead, she walked to the end of the mattress. Her bare feet were light on the cold cement, her heels black with dirt. She unbuttoned her shorts and tugged them down from her green panties. A fresh butterfly bandage was fixed above the scars on her thigh. Her pale legs, long for her small body, seemed to glow in the early light.

"When did that happen?" I asked softly.

"Just now," she said, lowering herself to sit on the edge of the mattress.

I was too afraid to ask why. Perhaps it was Leon—the fear and helplessness. Or perhaps it was me. She kept special bandages and a travel-sized bottle of antiseptic in her purse. When we were first together, she'd let me watch the fixing of one of her cuts. Perched on the lip of the bathtub, she spread antiseptic along the thin line of blood. She let it stand before unwrapping a bandage and smoothing it over the cut in a single motion. The precise, delicate ritual reminded me of watching my father shave. For a moment, I'd thought I understood: the hurting and the fixing of that hurt, not so different from punching out a TV screen.

I'd been sure I could make her stop.

She lay back on the rough green blanket. Three feet separated us. She twined her fingers over her breasts. They rose and fell. I didn't know how to lie beside her. What was allowed. I wanted to reach across and pull her toward me. I felt like I was still driving, like the whole screen porch was sliding across the earth, western states shrinking away in the rearview mirror.

I pulled my shirt over my head and tossed it into the corner. It landed in a clump beside our erupted suitcases.

Frantically packed clothes and bathroom supplies. The pile of Elli's underwear caught glimmers of sunlight. Shining forms. Sea creatures. Her eyes moved slowly from one corner of the ceiling to the other, as if she could see something I could not. A piece of our history, or connection to the wild earth.

Everything since we'd arrived was a blur: carrying Leon, tranquilized, through the night, the fluorescent bulb glaring over the steel operating table, Hutch—a bald little wire of a man—working the surgical tweezers deeper and deeper into Leon's flesh, while Elli sat beside him pale as death, until finally the tines reemerged triumphant, a squashed metal nub clenched between them. "Probably thought he had him in his sights but by the time he pulled the trigger all he got was a haunch," Hutch had said. "Coyotes are slippery."

Slippery. My hand rested on my own hip; a haunch seemed bad enough.

The tips of Elli's teeth shone between her parted lips. Hutch's boots squeaked on the linoleum inside the rusting trailer. He was on the phone canceling his morning appointments. Machine parts and the junked-out carcasses of old cars were silhouetted through the screen, like the remnants of a lost civilization. The entire acre was littered with junk—oil cans, traffic cones, warped rounds of chicken wire. What should have been the guest room was the infirmary, occupied by a pair of poisoned German shepherds. NO TRESPASSING signs were nailed to every other tree. At first I'd thought we must have the wrong address, that we'd pulled onto the property of a demented meth cook or neo-Nazi. One of the Redoubters, armed and barricaded against the government.

I caught a whiff of stale tobacco. Cigar butts covered the small table by the door. Elli's expression was both lost and focused. I touched my bare chest, the wiry hairs, dug my finger between my ribs. My heart beat: *alive, alive, alive.* I dropped my hand and rolled onto my elbow.

"We saved his life," I said. "That's twice now."

Her eyes stopped on a bent nail in the far corner. A single confused cricket sawed its bow in the morning sun. I couldn't keep my eyes from running over her legs: the dirty soles of her feet, reddish knees, the fresh bandage on her thigh, the green triangle of her underwear. She smelled sharp, of sterilizer. "You wanted him to die," she said.

"How can you say that?"

"You did." She paused. "I thought he was going to, too. I was so scared."

"It was a long drive. We were exhausted."

"I don't know what I would've done. I wanted to keep going north, all the way, until there was nowhere left to go."

Her shirt had bunched above her belly and her belly button was lighter than the skin around it. A strange blond pucker. I wondered if I'd ever put my finger in there. Were there parts of her I'd never touched? I could hardly remember what my life had been like before we met. "As soon as he's ready we'll go home," I said. "A day or two, at most."

Elli rolled her head over and looked at me sadly, like I was a little boy. "I'm staying here."

I shook my head. "Jen's covering for me tonight and tomorrow, I can't be gone any longer than that."

"He needs to heal. It's going to take time. Weeks, at least."

Something solid formed in my throat. I saw Leon's face, the smug look of contentment after she'd fed him, his amber eyes shining, the same look he had over the broken corpse of a cat. "We can take care of him at home, like always. He'll heal there with us."

"It's not safe. Hutch said I can help with the other animals. I've always wanted to . . . to . . ." She trailed off.

"To what?"

Her eyes cut across mine, warning me to keep my voice down. "I can't wait tables for the rest of my life."

Sunlight played across her collarbone. I bit my lower lip, focusing on the flash of pain. "We have a house," I answered. "A lease. You have *loans*." Hutch's boots were heavy on the linoleum floor inside, approaching and receding, a few of his words audible, "Acepromazine . . . swabs . . . no." Elli pressed her cheek into the pillow.

"And what's he going to pay you in?" I struggled to whisper. "Biscuits? Scraps of meat?"

Tears slid onto the white fabric of the pillowcase. "It's best for Leon."

"You want me to drive back alone? Is that right?" My elbow and shoulder were aching; my heart had begun to pound. Trying to squirm out from under a huge, thick-veined hand. The end comes slow and then very fast.

"I was hoping you could ship a few things. Warmer clothes, my computer." On her hip, above the scars she'd given herself, was a rounder, less uniform scar, where she'd been burned against our stove last Thanksgiving, struggling with yams. Our whole families had come: my dad and brother, her parents. As if we were real adults, a real couple. Not a pair of heart-wild kids who'd been thrown together and would surely part.

"No," I said. "Whatever it is, we can fix it. We can make it work."

She turned away and her hair fell back, showing the full length of her neck, the delicate tremble of her pulse. Red imperfections flecked the skin on her chest. She looked up toward the slanting sunlight. She was small enough that I could have picked her up and run with her into the woods. Crashing through the underbrush, deeper and deeper, branches whipping our cheeks and blocking out the sun, her body light in my arms. My feet going to paws, fur springing from my neck. Away from the trailer and the cars and the roads, the hunters, my life, the whole wanting world.

Would she love me then?

I scooted across the blanket and pressed my hips against hers. I draped my arm over her shoulder. "Elli."

"Rye." She pushed my arm away. "Please don't make this harder."

DADDY SWORE AN OATH

"MOM!" THE VOICE CAME FROM FAR AWAY. LILA REALIZED SHE was sitting on the kitchen floor. How had she gotten there? True stood buck-naked, dripping, in the doorway. His scrawny arms and hairless chest pink from the bathwater, hair pasted on his forehead, a wild, vengeful look in his eyes. "Otis took my speedboat. Make him give it back."

Lila pushed up through the heavy curtain. Moved her lips. "What time is it?" Her butt was cold on the linoleum and a cabinet handle stabbed her back. She brushed her hair from her eyes. Patted the back of her skull to make sure it wasn't cracked. The hell kind of a single mother would she be? "You have school."

True stared at her. "I know that." His face slowly registered the strangeness of his mother on the floor. He forgot the toy, the injustice. Fear flickered in his eyes. "What're you doing?"

"Get dressed," Lila said. She pulled herself up by the edge of the counter. Stood unsteadily. Snow had begun to fall outside the kitchen window, as if she didn't have enough to worry about. She bunched her fists in the sides of her sweatpants. Swore that if one more shitstorm landed on her head, just one more, she'd give it all up and move with the boys back to her parents' place in Tucson.

Drops of water clung to True's eyelashes. Long, like little wisps of fear themselves. She crossed the kitchen and drew his bony shoulders to her waist. His cheek-warmth passed through her tatty T-shirt to her stomach. For the past two weeks, she'd felt she was looking life right in its bloodshot, shifty eye, but still the fresh smell that rose off him was nearly enough to make her cry. She scratched his wet head. Flopped his shoulders back. "Go on, now, you and your brother both. I'm making waffles."

He peered behind her, disturbed but enticed. "Chocolate chip?"

She nodded. "You can't be running around here naked, not now." She wiped her eyes. A white news van was parked down the block, nearly invisible in the snow. It had been there three days, since Lane Lemus got killed trying to leave the Little Charbonneau Wildlife Refuge, and Lila's husband posted a video online: "*There are no laws in these United States anymore. This is a free-for-all. Patriots, stand up. If they try to stop you from getting here, any L.E.O. or military or feds, shoot them.*"

Shoot them? *Shoot them?* Christ. Lila believed in what her husband was doing, but she hadn't realized he was willing to die for it. That he was willing to leave her, and the boys, behind. True shivered, turned, and dashed up the stairs, spraying water on the carpeted landing. "Slow down!" Lila yelled. His little pink foot was the last thing to disappear. Children were so delicate. You never thought of that until you had one, then you couldn't think of anything else. The month before, she'd found True atop a left-out ladder—Briar careless with his projects—wobbling and reaching skyward, with that idiotic, boyish look of exhilaration on his face. When she'd gotten him down and had him in her arms again, she couldn't believe he was alive. She'd lived his arcing fall and splattered death so many times in the few seconds between.

She went to the fridge and dug around the freezer, finding the waffles behind a rock-hard slab of a bison Briar had shot. The microwave beeped at her as she pushed the buttons. She jabbed them, trying to shake the feelings of bright and closing doom. Who had let Briar in front of the camera, anyway? It should've been one of the rich ones, the ranchers. With their careful cowboy drawls, talking about liberty and peaceful armed protest, like Thomas Jefferson himself was blowing on their balls. So she could sleep at night, and not be fainting in her own damn kitchen. The falling snow through the window reminded her of a screen saver. Flat, repetitive, endless. She poured the chocolate chips onto the waffles and slammed the plastic door. Replaced the box in the freezer, and had a sudden urge to fling the bison meat out into the snow, as if the beast might regrow itself there, amble off, and forgive the man who'd killed it.

Forgiveness from meat. A bad sign. Fresh dizziness made her lean against the counter. She remembered the night it all started: Briar's knuckles white in front of the TV as he watched the Drummond brothers being taken away in handcuffs, for grazing on land that their family had used for a hundred years. Now set aside to protect the northern pintail and tundra swan. His fearful rage, out in the garage yelling on the phone, cursing, banging the supplies he stockpiled around. In the morning, he'd told her he was driving to Harney County in eastern Oregon, where they were being held.

"Who's going to be next?" he'd said, when she tried to stop him.

Sometimes she wished she'd married an accountant. Or Kevin Cox, her first boyfriend, who now managed a hardware store in Flagstaff. A nice town, full of trees. He probably had a whole house there. Not a duplex like this one, lopped in half, Mrs. Grevit stomping around on the other side of the thin walls. But Lila was proud of Briar, too. He was a man of principle, always had been, and even if taking over a wildlife refuge wasn't how she'd have shown it, what of all the others in their hunting caps in the McDonald's drive-through? Or sulking in front of the TV at Jackie's Bar? Moaning and complaining about the government but doing nothing. Like her sister's husband, who didn't even stand up when you came in the room, and looked like he'd been squeezed into his khakis through a tube.

True and Otis jostled into the kitchen. Otis had his shirt on backward, as usual. Lila ordered him over and wrestled it off his arms. He struggled against her, flailing his elbows, wanting to watch the chocolate chips melt and ooze through the microwave's glowing window. "Stop it, *Ma*," he said.

RIGGINS' LONE SNOWPLOW had beaten Lila onto Tucker Street. She drove in the sweep of cleared pavement. The windshield wipers slapped away falling flakes. She envied the wipers. Wanted to get out and do some slapping herself. The snowbank at the curb was already three feet high. Soon people would have to use shovels to dig out their cars. Why anyone wanted to live in this frigid place was beyond her. Before meeting Briar, the farthest north she'd been was Las Vegas. They'd come to Idaho to be closer to his family and other like-minded people in the heart of the Redoubt, a defensible strip of country two hundred miles long, from Garden Valley to White Bird, and stretching east into the Frank Church–River of No Return Wilderness, with the Wallowa and Bitterroot Mountains as natural borders. Attracting more newcomers every year. Their church and school were full of Constitutionalists, and the sheriff had sworn not to enforce any illegal laws, but what good were liberty and Christian values if it was too cold to leave the house? Lila smiled to herself. She felt she'd been taken on a long ride, and, in all the excitement, hadn't had time to wonder if she wanted to get off.

Ahead, a blue Camaro fishtailed at the stoplight on Grove

Street. "He must be stupid," True said, buckled in to the backseat.

She agreed silently as they passed the Freedom Bank and Sunrise Café. Who else would buy a Camaro in Idaho? She felt more solid now that they were in the truck, in motion. This was her, and this was her life. Any reckoning just now would lead to misery. A few people bustled between the doors of the single row of brick buildings downtown. Shop owners shoveled the sidewalks. "Stupid, stupid, stupid," Otis parroted, sending the word ricocheting through Lila's brain. She didn't have the energy to chastise him. Four cops stood outside the courthouse in puffy blue coats. They followed the truck with their eyes, and she wondered if they knew who she was.

Sally Winder was directing traffic in her neon-yellow crossing guard vest in front of the elementary school. She'd put on so much weight since her father died it surprised Lila she could still do the job. Seeing the truck, Sally's whole face reddened, and she waddled and slipped through the snow to the driver's window. Holding up her right hand to halt traffic, she made a rolling-down motion with her left.

"I been praying for you," she panted through the crack, cold air streaming in along with her words.

The boys went quiet and still in the back. People had been telling Lila they were praying for her for weeks now and she still didn't know how to respond. "Thanks," she said.

"How are you? You heard anything? All I see on the news are the feds and that crooked sheriff. Seems they won't even let them talk anymore."

Lila nodded. Felt the line of cars growing behind her.

"It's a cover-up. The whole thing. They're killing people and sweeping it under the rug. I never thought I'd see it. My dad, if he was still around, he'd be out there." Sally jerked her fat chin, as if sending forth his vengeful ghost. "You mark my words."

"I know he would," Lila said.

Sally paused. "If I hadn't married such an ass." She shook her head, bits of snow tumbling down her round cheeks. A horn honked. "You come over to the church this week, you hear? There are so many people who are thinking about you. Who are with you."

Sure, Lila thought, *with her* but staying put. All the Oath-keepers and Three Percenters and militias. In their warm safe houses and warm safe church meetings, while Briar was in a tent somewhere (she didn't even know where exactly any-more, since they'd had to evacuate the refuge's visitors center) with a circle of guns pointed at him. Everyone was so good at talking and posting articles and then going on with their lives. None of the so-called like-minded she knew had heeded Briar's call. Was it cowardice? Or oblivion? Or did they love their families more? She squeezed the steering wheel, trying to force away the thought.

The horn honked again. Lila realized it was likely snowing in Oregon, too. Only two hundred miles from here, in the Jordan Valley, with the Pillars of Rome blazing in the dis-tance. She wondered what food he and the others had left. If the generator was holding out. How his face looked at that exact moment: the length of his beard, the lines around his light blue eyes. Sally stared in at her, wanting something more, an illicit detail, hint of bloodshed to come. "We better get along," Lila said. "Bell's about to ring."

Reluctantly, Sally stepped aside. "I'll be praying."

Lila rolled her window up and eased the truck through the intersection to the curb in front of the main doors. Children were streaming inside in scarlet hats and scarves, bright as chili peppers, their cheeks flushed from the cold, waving to parents gathered on the sidewalk. Another everyday. Lila wanted to scream at them to wake up. To look around and see what was happening. The only thing that seemed to have changed was her life. Every crazed minute of it. She took a deep breath and looked in the rearview mirror. True and Otis were leaned together in the backseat, staring up at her. Otis had a looseness around his lips like he was about to cry. She wondered what the other boys had been saying in school. Kids that age were capable of a boundless cruelty.

"People just love your dad a lot," Lila said. "And they get worked up sometimes, like I do. That's all."

"Mom?" Otis said.

"He's safe," she lied. "I promise. He'll be home soon."

THE NEWS VAN sat still and silent—a mound in the snow. It was parked half a block down from the duplex, but still where Lila figured they could see in through the windows. She pulled into the driveway, wondering where the crew had gone. She pictured them in one of the fancy hotels in Nampa, drinking martinis and laughing, waiting out the storm. The bloodsuckers.

She got out and trudged past the garage. Inside were Briar's two snowmobiles. He'd told her to sell the older one if money got desperate, but it had PATRIOT scrawled in red paint across the cowling, which couldn't help the resale value. Snow was falling so heavily that the boys' small footprints were already filled in on the front walk. Lila didn't have the energy to get the shovel. Maybe this way, Mrs. Grevit would fall and break something and freeze to death. Lila muttered a prayer for forgiveness at the thought—*not now*—and stamped the snow off her boots on the welcome mat.

The silence of the living room was a shock at first. The boys were only nine and seven, but they made the noise of small hurricanes. A rattle in the air, even when they slept. Lila took off her coat and stood in the empty room. Dust motes settled in the corners. Briar had warned her it might be bugged. She pictured FBI agents in a surveillance van somewhere, listening to her children tear-assing around and squalling whenever she tried to make them put on clothes. She thought of lying down on the carpet and staring at the ceiling until she went to sleep. She could vaguely remember a time when a nap had been a solution. An hour gone and the world reset, whatever had upset her forgotten. It still worked for Otis, but True . . . She shook her head, walked into the kitchen, and finished washing the dishes.

Upstairs, she gathered the sopping towels from the bathroom floor. A scum of soap and dirt covered the water in the undrained tub. True's anger over the red speedboat already felt like another lifetime. It floated upside down next to a yellow duck. Little animals. She smiled without meaning to, reached in, pulled the plug, and watched the water and whatever residue of them it held slowly swirl away. The picture came to her of a winter morning a few years before, when Briar had taken a bath along with the boys. All three of them in this little tub. She'd sat on the toilet lid handing over toys and washcloths but mostly being ignored. She wondered if she'd ever be so happy again.

Even if the feds kicked down the door, took every gun from the house, and fitted her with a tracking collar, she wouldn't leave True and Otis. That was the difference between fathers and mothers: fathers could leave. "I'm doing it for them," Briar had said, from the window of his truck, and she'd nodded. She'd actually *nodded*, like he was goddamned Paul Revere. Now she didn't know if someone would call if he got shot, or if she'd find out on the news like everyone else.

Unconsciously, she took her phone from her pocket. Still an hour before work. No messages. She went downstairs and made coffee. Ate half a piece of bread. The dry crumbs were tasteless on her tongue, another chore. Nothing made her angrier than the TV women who talked about motherhood as if it were a feast for the senses, a lush delight. Sometimes Lila completely forgot what her body looked like. Realized she hadn't had an un-microwaved meal in weeks. Large white flakes continued to fall through the window, covering everything in the backyard: the slide, the sandbox, softening all the hard edges and putting the trash cans to sleep. Lila could see where the word *blanketed* came from. Like God tossing down a great white quilt and then turning away. She let herself fantasize about a day off: all those hours alone to do whatever she wanted. But where would her mind go? The thought turned frightening. It was better to work, to keep moving. She'd told Briar she could handle things here, and she intended to make good on that promise, at least.

Often, after the boys went to bed, she turned on CNN, muted it, and watched for hours, waiting for a glimpse of his face. The national news hardly covered the growing unrest— never mentioning land rights, pretending it didn't exist—but once in a while he appeared on-screen in an old interview, and a protective feeling rushed through her chest so strong she was tempted to take the pistol from the bedside drawer, load the boys in the car, and drive to him through the night. His head was surprisingly egg shaped in the upward tilt of the cameras, bald dome gleaming, the lower half covered in scruff. In real life, she was taller than him, and was used to looking down on the wide bones of his forehead. She wondered if she'd ever see him from above again, outside of a coffin.

SPORTSMAN'S WAREHOUSE was fifteen miles south of Riggins, by the New Meadows Airport. The roads were a mess: traffic backed up behind accidents, snowdrifts spilling across intersections. The golf course was a long, unbroken plain of white.

It took Lila nearly forty minutes to get there, and she was late. Cursing, she parked at the edge of the lot. She recognized the few other cars as her coworkers'. Checking her makeup in the rearview mirror, she gathered her lunch and purse and hurried through the snow to the store. It was insanity to her that she still had to work, but the boys still had to eat, and Briar was doing his résumé no favors. Would he ever be able to get a job again? Lila closed her eyes in front of the sliding glass doors and listened to them hiss open. She was greeted by the sharp, familiar scent of new plastic, and the expanse of clothes, boots, skis, bicycles, bows, and guns.

Basketball hoops loomed overhead. She touched her hair, making sure it was still in place, and again thought aimlessly of the regrown bison. Barreling down the aisles, crashing through protein powder displays, butting a hole in the dressing room wall. It sounded good to her. She'd much rather spend the day patching plaster than telling customers about smart-wool technology, grip wax versus glide wax.

Greg Harrison was waiting for her in the staff room, his blue manager's polo neatly ironed, drinking coffee beneath the Employee Activity Board—mostly pictures of the owner's grinning Mormon family jet-boating on Lake Lowell, like the end of the world couldn't come soon enough. Lila started to apologize but Greg waved her off. "Nobody here anyway. Should be slow all day. I'll keep you on the floor."

"Thanks." This was a kindness. There were lots of places to hide on the floor, shelves to pretend to straighten, clothes to refold. Unlike the register, where all you could do was stand

and stare. She guessed Greg was a liberal—he'd gone to the University of Washington and wore tight-fitting jeans—but he'd been kind to her through the whole ordeal, always asking if she needed any help, any time off.

"We're going to have to start stocking hot toddies to get anyone in if this snow keeps up." He smiled and the little mole on his neck quivered. Lila smiled back, until she noticed something new in his eyes. A gleam, maybe, as if he were sizing her up. It was the first time it occurred to her that she might become single again. What that would mean. Loneliness. Dating. Explaining new men to the boys. Someone like Greg seeing her body for the first time after she'd twice given birth. Feeling nauseated, she turned and carried her lunch to the fridge.

The store remained empty through the afternoon, even after the snow stopped. Lila spent most of her shift by the sleeping bags, repacking the nylon and microfiber and fleece, memorizing the warmth ratings, inspecting the wash instructions on the little tags. Greg watched her from behind the gun counter, his eyes following her from row to row. She imagined pulling one of the bags over her head, all the way down, so only her feet poked out and she was enveloped by a warm dark cocoon. Staying there for hours. What a pretty, stupid thought. She counted down the minutes, worrying about the boys at school, and if her mother-in-law would be on time to pick them up. The rifles and shotguns hanging above Greg's head threatened to blow the ceiling full of holes. But then at least he might've looked away.

DEBRA LEE DIGGS stood in a pocket of blazing light on the front stoop, her left hand on True's shoulder, her right on Otis's, her wide, wrinkled face fixed in an expression of stoic worry beneath her bottle-blond hair. The cameraman crouched before her on the front walk. He'd cleared a place in the snow to brace himself. The camera's light was so bright it captured not only Debra Lee and the boys but also the reporter, whose makeup-caked cheeks had a plastic sheen, as if she were only part real. A doll coming to life. She looked stunned, holding the microphone up as Debra Lee spoke.

White-hot anger surged through Lila's chest. She swerved the truck to a stop. The word *bitch* repeated in her head—*bitch, bitch, bitch*—like an ax chopping through heavy wood. She jumped out, slammed the door, and made straight for the stoop. Debra Lee went silent, her mouth open, as if she'd forgotten her English. The reporter repeated her question. I'm going to kill her, Lila thought. Murder. Straight up.

A producer intercepted her in the yard. "Mrs. Diggs," he said.

"Get away from my house," she answered.

The producer raised his hands. "Please, she gave us permission. We have waivers."

"My kids, too?" Lila thought of shoving him. He was a small, mouselike man. He'd go down easy. His coat hung off him like a hanger. Instead, she took a step to the side, planning to barrel straight for Debra Lee, lower her shoulder, sweep up the boys.

"This is live," the producer said. "Just so you know, anything you do—it's live."

The word took a moment to register, but it held Lila in place. She would cause a scene. Hysterical wife of crazed militiaman. The clip would get picked up by other networks, national networks, loop endlessly on the Internet. Briar wouldn't want that. Lila clenched her fists and waited, her breath billowing in front of her.

The producer shifted from foot to foot as if he were about to scurry away. "A nation of slaves . . . we have to say no peacefully . . . don't take everything you hear about my son . . . my son." Debra Lee's words floated up to the dark sky, and then out to, what, ten thousand TV sets? Twenty, thirty? Who was watching her boys right now? Who might come for them in the night?

When the interview was finished, Lila shouldered past the cameraman, crossed the yard, and knelt on the stoop. She kissed True on the cheek and Otis on the forehead. Their small faces confused her anger and left her feeling helpless. "Go on upstairs," she said. "I need to talk to your nana."

"Were we on TV?" Otis asked.

She nodded and smiled. "You did great. Now get on inside."

The smile clung to her face as she stood. It felt rigid and horrible. She turned to Debra Lee, squared her shoulders, and tried to find words. "Just what in the hell do you think you're doing?"

"Don't use that language," Debra Lee said. "Not now."

Lila stared at her mother-in-law. She had the smashed

face of a bulldog, a slug. Her fried hair was tragic. They'd moved up here to be close to *this*? The news crew backed away down the walk and began packing up their gear. "I don't care who you talk to or what kind of a fool you make of yourself," Lila hissed. "But you have no right to put my boys on camera."

Debra Lee huffed and pushed through the door into the warmth of the living room. "They need to know what a hero their father is. What he's doing."

Lila followed, shutting and locking the door behind her. "They know."

"People need to see them. I don't think the way you're hiding out here—"

"Hiding out?"

"They need to know you're real, we're real people. Real *Americans*. And they're taking our rights. They're killing peaceful protesters." Debra Lee looked older in the dim light, her body a squat rectangle on the carpet. "This whole country needs to rise up."

"So, what, I should be bringing the boys on *The Today Show*, crying?"

"It might help." Debra Lee looked at her defiantly, then turned away, her shoulders sagging. "They won't cover it otherwise."

Briar was her only son. It had taken an operation to have him, and more than once Lila'd heard her call him her miracle. Lila figured this was what gave him his oversized self-confidence, but now, knowing her own boys were listening from the top of the stairs, the fire in her chest began to cool.

"Don't worry about watching them tomorrow," she said. "I'm taking the day off."

AFTER A DINNER of meatballs and ketchup on hot dog buns—Otis's favorite—Lila had both boys get into their pajamas. Swaddled in blankets and huddled together on the living room couch, she read to them from *Little Survivors: Life in the Woods*, a picture book their father had gotten for them, which they now wanted to hear every night. They listened as the brothers Thomas and George learned to dig a pit trap, and how to take cover if they heard a drone. When their father was shot by a corrupt federal agent, he promised to watch over them from the sky. Otis sucked in his breath.

"Is that like Daddy?" he asked.

"No," True said, before Lila could answer. "Why are you always so stupid?"

"*True*," Lila said. Otis began to cry. She looked up at the ceiling and shut the book. "It's not stupid. That is like your dad. Except he's alive, too. So he's watching over you in real life."

"But they want to kill him," True said.

Lila turned, finding his light blue eyes, mirrors of his father's, fixed on her face. "What do you mean?"

"Jackson said so at school. He said the FBI wants to kill my dad and the other people he's with, but he didn't know why."

"Well, he's wrong. Nobody wants to kill anybody. Do you remember what your dad said before he left? To both of you?"

Otis was silent, curled in a tight ball.

"He said he swore an oath," True said.

"That's right. He swore an oath to uphold the Constitution. That's all he's doing."

But Lila knew it was more than that. Everything on the news had made Briar furious. She'd had to marshal their dinner conversations like a talk show host, cars and sports, keep it bland and chirpy, or else he'd explode and spend an hour on Muslim sleeper cells along the East Coast, cartels controlling the border, or Sharia law on university campuses. It wasn't only about the Drummonds, and their cattle lands, not really. He was fighting a world that had changed out from underneath him.

Next door, Mrs. Grevit's TV was blaring, though mercifully a sitcom. Lila was determined to keep the boys from watching, or hearing, the news. If something happened to Briar, they'd find out from her. She smoothed her hand over Otis's forehead, feeling his small heat. The knocking engine within.

LILA LAY IN BED and stared at the ceiling. She wondered where the bugs would be if the FBI had hidden them. The light fixtures, maybe. She was too tired to check. The clock on the bedside table ticked toward midnight. Her phone lay beside it. She closed her eyes. Fears and memories sped through her mind like a movie on fast forward, too jerky and disjointed to follow. After a while, she sat up and switched on the lamp. She looked over at the small TV on the dresser. No. Not tonight. Picked up an old copy of *Us Weekly* and paged through the actresses and pop singers and reality stars. Getting coffee, walking their dogs, living their comfortable, meaningless lives. Then a two-page spread of Summer Bodies. Bikini-clad women running from the waves. She threw the magazine aside and lay back.

An engagement photo of her and Briar hung on the far wall. Both of them facing the camera, her hair up, his arms wrapped around her waist, the dark Marine blue of his uniform starched stiff across his shoulders. She remembered the firmness of his hands, his chest pressed against her back, breath hot on her neck. After the photo was taken, the photographer had left the room and Briar had slid his hand up the inside of her thigh, squeezing her skin, kissing and biting her collarbone with a sudden urgency, as if he needed to both love and destroy her.

He'd said they'd always be together. That it was just the two of them in the whole world. She wondered if she was more of a fool than any other woman.

The heater ticked. The sky outside was pure black. Sixteen days it had been since he left, almost seventeen. Two and a half weeks of no touch, no comfort. No joy, no pleasure. Lila remembered nights—after a stupid fight or wrong word—when she'd wanted nothing more than for him to be gone from this bed. She laid her hand flat on her bare stomach. She felt like she was on the brink of discovering just how strong she was, but she didn't want to. She pictured Briar in his tent—the same one they'd camped in from the Grand Canyon to the Beartooths—awake also, his light blue eyes glinting beneath his heavy brow in the gleam of stars. She moved her fingers along the top seam of her panties. She tried to send a telepathic message. *I need you more than they do.*

But did she? She closed her eyes and thought of the way he shifted his weight onto her after turning off the light. The wiry scrape of his chest hair, thick fingers on her neck. Her mind traced outward, to Kevin Cox in his parents' basement, his hands shaking, her jeans unzipped, then to Cole Lenihan whom she'd dated briefly while working at a gas station, his hair an oddly perfect blond bowl, his gangly height his greatest attraction. Even Greg, watching her endlessly. She let her hand slide down. If the FBI was listening they could go straight to hell. The room seemed to soften, and stretch. Her fingers moved. Her muscles relaxed. She imagined unfamiliar lips against hers, a reckless tongue, a country singer, a complete stranger. Kissing down her chest and stomach and then looking up from between her legs, needing some confirmation, *Yes*, like a lost boy. Her favorite moment.

Outside in the street, a car door slammed, and Lila's hand froze. Her whole body went stiff. The room was silent for a moment, save for the tick of the heater, then footsteps crunched in the snow on the front walk. The hairs on her arms stood up. She yanked her hand from beneath the blanket. A wave of fear and shame crashed down on her. Go away, she prayed. Please. Just keep going.

The front gate whined open. She realized, in a burst of panic, that her action, her sin, had led directly to Briar's death. Shots had rang out while she . . . while she did *what?* She saw a tent—their tent—riddled with holes. Blood pooling on the snow. The electric light of a flash grenade as the feds stormed in.

It was impossible, even if . . . it was too soon. But Lila felt the first cuts of a guilt from which she feared she might never recover.

NEWS VANS BLOCKED the road in both directions. The dawn was ice-clear, the Wallowa Mountains visible in the distance, their jagged bulk rising unfeeling from the flatlands. Reporters stood clumped between the snowbanks in front of the ncighbors' house. Streams of their breath twisted together. Red and blue lights silently flashed atop the police cruiser at the end of the block.

Lila stood at the window. She clasped her hands in front of her stomach. A dull pain throbbed behind her right eye. She hadn't slept. She hadn't told the boys. She'd sat on her bed in the dark since the men left, as if, were she not to move, if she stayed perfectly still, things would go back to the way they'd been before.

But now she was up, and a hard fury had formed in her chest. She knew she'd never feel safe again. They'd taken that from her, along with everything else. The reporters watched the duplex, stamping their feet for warmth. The boys would be waking up soon. Her mind traveled back across sleepless nights, laughter, shouting, a wedding, two births . . . Snuffed out, for what?

Her hands began to shake. She went to the mirror above the dresser. She started to wipe the tears from her cheeks, then stopped. It was better to leave the salty streaks. Let people see. She pulled her hair back tightly into a ponytail, exposing the blotched paleness of her cheeks, her bloodshot eyes. She smoothed the strands back above her ears. She was a neighbor, a mother. An American. A widow.

She buttoned her blouse. Taking a last breath, she drew herself up to her full height. Here it was, the final shitstorm. She walked from the room and down the stairs to the front door.

The freezing outside air struck her like a fist. Reporters rushed forward in a slipping thicket, microphones and phones and cameras extended. Lila's first instinct was to slam the door. Stumble back inside, cry, pray. Hide out with the boys and then move to the desert where no one would know their name.

No. She dug her nails into the meat of her palm, and stepped into the cold.

The street was silent for a moment, a great wave of expectation building, then Lila opened her mouth and all at once the reporters spoke, *"Mrs. Diggs." "Mrs. Diggs." "Mrs. Diggs."*

COME DOWN TO THE
WATER

WE WERE ALL AT HAL'S CABIN ON DICKEY LAKE MAKING MUD
grenades and trying to blow up the dock when Carston and
his girl pulled in. Hal, Jensen, Cap, Till, and me. We'd been
coming since we were kids. The bank had foreclosed on the
property and Hal had urged us up to do final damage.

"Nothing but Mormons now anyhow," he said, nodding at
the buzz-cut lawns on either side of his family's mangy hill.
He had a beer in one hand and the mud-covered M-80 in his
other was fast reaching its potential. I was out of work, had
been for months, so none of it mattered to me. He heaved the
rocket toward the neighbor's woodpile.

Carston and his girl walked up right at the bang and she
threw her hands over her ears, so the first thing we saw was

the withered one dangling from the left side of her head like it had grown there. The right number of fingers but a size too small, sagged together, and mostly boneless. Like a claw, if it weren't so helpless.

Red sparks showered the stacked logs and disappeared.

Nearly busting with pride, Carston introduced her as Sara, resting his hand on the back of her neck. She was a full foot shorter than him and looked nervous but content in his shadow. Her brown hair was pulled tightly back from her pale forehead. I gave her an awkward squeeze, trying to be polite and pretend we were the types who hugged at first meeting. She smelled the way college girls do: like incense and pot and good soap, even if they don't use it very often.

Hal was next, and, twisted up with anger over the loss of his cabin, he leaned in to practically sniff the appendage. She tucked it into the pocket of her dress. Smoke hung in the dry afternoon air.

Turning from her, I found myself with my arms around Carston's broad sweaty shoulders, smelling the sour-milk smell that had always polluted his family's trailer. We'd never had much reason for being friends other than the fact that we were both from the easternmost row of Clear Creek Trailer Court in Eureka. Or, to put it right, he'd never had much reason to be friends with me. A chunk was still missing from his nose where I'd shot him with a BB gun. He hadn't even cried. Just stared at me, blood running down his chin, the Barbie doll sitting on his head wobbling, and the next day I was clean forgiven.

Seeing him and Sara was a reminder of his goodness. He was better than me. Better than most of us. Giving and forgiving and turning his cheek so many ways I always figured he'd end up killed or in the nuthouse. If I had to run the percentages, I'd say he was in the top three or four worldwide, right behind the mahatmas and the holy sisters. The question of his goodness was one I'd long tangled with, for around that pure heart was a big, sweaty, stinking, ugly body.

"If we'd known you were coming we'd have thrown down some hay in the barn," Hal said.

"Filled the trough with slop." That was Jensen, Hal's fat snively little echo. The Bic lighter he'd been using had the safety torn off so when he sparked it the flame shot up a good six inches. He waved it at Carston's nose.

"We're getting married." Carston beamed, as if the insults were the perfect setup for the big news he'd been carrying in his pocket. He slung his arm around Sara's shoulders. She shifted her feet to bear the weight. He grinned at me, his wide features flattening below his buzz cut, holding the words out like the dinosaur teeth we used to find in Black Coulee.

"I'll be damned," I said. The urge to settle down had struck me lately, too, though I had no takers, and it was a deep pang of envy that caught me seeing the way they leaned together in the sunlight coming off the lake.

I pictured them in coitus, his paws hanging off the white marriage bed. She was a small girl, not frail but petite, with a thinness at her joints, particularly the wrist down by her withered hand. She'd have to be on top just to survive. Her body did nice things to her red-and-white-checked dress. I only had to close half an eye to think old Carston had done all right for himself.

Cap and his twin brother Till came up from the blackened dock. They were smoke jumpers, built like trees, and saw no irony in tossing pyrotechnics on their off weeks.

"Uglier than ever," Cap said, gripping Carston's hand. He did a start when he saw Sara's. The smile she gave showed she was used to it and it would be a hard thing to break through her grace, though I had a feeling that before the day was out one of us would find a way.

"We met in Missoula," Carston said. "She's getting her degree."

"Well, hell, your critters might have half a brain between them." I smiled at Sara, hoping to put myself right. I saw future sloe-eyed children with who knows what for limbs.

"I got a degree." Hal leaned forward. "A degree in getting fucked by people with degrees."

He went on from there, his cheeks red with booze, his scruffy chin jabbing the air, about Missoula's queers and how most of them worked in banks, and the Mormons and their tar-sands money, and how his great-grandpa had built this cabin back when all you could see onshore were a couple of goddamn tepees. It was quite a speech and pretty much brought the happy couple up to speed.

Sara stood in the grass with her good hand on Carston's elbow, a worried expression hiding behind her smile. Carston just beamed. One of the reasons I'd chosen him to shoot in the face, besides his being so big and good, was that he acted like all of us he'd grown up with were just characters in a movie. If we spat or said terrible things or stabbed each other, the scene would cut and we'd all be stitched up right as new. I'd wanted to prove him wrong, but even losing a nostril hadn't changed him.

Till suggested drinks, so we filed onto the porch, where the big cooler lay sprawled open, piled with ice and cans of beer. We'd brought the fishing gear out thinking we'd take the boat in the evening. Not likely, the way we were getting set. The rods and nets were tangled against the moldy shingle siding and someone had knocked over the bait. Till handed out beers, stomping the fleeing wigglers with his Wolverines.

I sat on the picnic table. The cedar top was cracked where long ago Hal had proved he could punch the hardest. Part of his knuckle was likely still gristled in between the splinters. Sara took the seat next to me. The M-80 smoke had cleared and her smell came on even stronger. She tucked her hand back in the pocket of her dress. There was only the one pocket on the left side, and I supposed she'd sewn it on special.

"Carston talks about you so much," she said.

"That right?"

She nodded. "He says you did most everything together." With that hand tucked away and all the pale skin on her throat and shoulders and the gentle turn of her lips, I was getting more jealous by the second.

"It's true, we were neighbors, the same age." I shrugged. "We did all kinds of running around."

She looked toward where he was sitting, gesturing happily with a beer that looked very small in his paw. Her eyes shone. "Was he always like this?"

"Well, he used to have a whole nose. Before I shot half of it off."

Her eyes widened. "He never told me that."

Of course he hadn't. I backed off, not wanting to darken her blush. "It was an accident. Just horsing around. I mistook him for a bear."

She laughed. The afternoon heat was gathering. It shimmered on the surface of the lake. I drank down most of my beer—grown warm, nearly foul—and wiped my mouth with the back of my hand.

"How'd you two meet?"

"It's embarrassing." She paused, as if she weren't going to tell me, though both of us knew she would. "I was sick. Outside a bar. He took care of me."

That sounded right. Saint Carston holding back her hair, wiping the chunks and yellow bits from her chin. His big hands holding her steady. How could she help but let him take her home? The others were still on the Mormons and queers, with Cap goading Hal to keep him going, Jensen stabbing worms with a sharpened twig, and Till just staring off into the hazy distance.

"His mom told me he used to pour milk on chicken nuggets and eat them like cereal." Sara's eyes sparkled, as if meeting Carston's refrigerator of a mother were some accomplishment. But what she said was true, damned if I hadn't seen it.

WE DRANK AWAY the afternoon and it became a celebration. The dangerous kind, when one thing is beginning and another ending. Hal invited some of his friends from the roofing trade. Big reservation boys, they came to drink, and when they heard our plans for the dock they took a sledgehammer down to the water and the dock was no more.

Sara would've left hours before were it not for Carston's beaming. But by evening she was drunk, too, and beside herself, unused to our practice of keeping our cans full with whiskey, vodka, moonshine, even mouthwash when all else ran out. She was from Oregon where maybe they had more sense.

It turned into a black and swirling night, and one way or another Hal was determined to have a time. "Hoorah," he kept saying, bumping me with his forearm.

The Indians dragged up the dock wood, doused it in gasoline, and made a bonfire. Twenty feet high at the peak, crackling and leaping toward the stars. Jensen did a drunk, jerking rain dance around it, and I laughed and laughed when the Indians knocked him down. He thrashed his stubby arms in the dust and they kept him there with their boots. Of course it was Carston who stepped in, afraid they were serious about rolling him into the flames.

Hal took a bottle of vodka and settled on an old plastic lawn chair. He looked out across the dark lake, up to his cabin, then at the fire. Glowering. Murderous. I moved away. I'd seen him throw a handle at a retriever when he got like that, and besides, I didn't want to hear any more about the bank or the

Latter Days. I found Sara on the deck and sat beside her, my arm up on the wet cooler.

I asked her about Missoula and she spoke of her studies and the places she'd been: Italy, Prague, Paris. From the way she told it, all these foreign countries were nothing but Gothic churches and cobblestone squares. "I was homesick most of the time," she said. "Even though it was so beautiful."

The firelight turned threads of her hair gold. I nodded, trying to act like I'd seen more of the world than the wind-blighted prairies of the Hi-Line and a seedy stretch of the Baja Peninsula where my mom took me one spring after a keno jackpot. She'd gotten so sunburned on the first day it was a miracle she had any skin left, ending our family vacations once and forever.

"Rome was so crowded I could hardly breathe," Sara said.

Across from us, Jensen lurched around the fire drinking vodka and Sprite from a gas can and cheering while Cap and Till wrestled in the moonlit grass. Cap got on top, bolted his knee around Till's neck, and rocked his pelvis against his chin, calling him a cocksucker. Till's face turned purple as he tried to squirm free.

Sara hardly seemed to notice the brothers in the grass, she was so deep in her memories. She kept talking, and as if by its own volition, her withered hand crept from her pocket and roamed the front of her dress. I guess it had gotten drunk, too, and frisky. I watched the hand journey across the red and white squares before alighting in the warm rift between her thighs. And while she spoke of some basilica I was captivated by the thought of that little creature on her bareness, what exactly it could do.

"Come with me," I interrupted. "Let me take you home." It was half a joke at all her talking, but if she'd stood up I would've found my keys. Goodness and friendship be goddamned.

She laughed. "He told me how sweet you were. That you'd make me feel at home."

I kept one eye on her little hand and used the other to nod, as if I were everything he'd said I was. A churchman, rising for the lights. She went quiet. Her eyes flicked across the dark shoreline and found Carston's shape by the boat shed.

STARLIGHT CAME TO PASS. Hal rose from his decrepit throne and long-shadowed across the grass. Sparks shot and crackled from the fire. He stood before it, a general in net shorts and an oversized T-shirt with the sleeves chewed off. He flexed his biceps and spat into the flames. Thorned tattoos coiled around his bare arms. They went all the way down his chest to his dick and ended there in a viny mess around the base. I'd seen it, against my will, when the ink was fresh and he new-father proud. Carston ambled up to his side, grinning and babbling about decades of friendship, old friends, small towns, the ones who know you best. That selfsame horseshit that kept us and our kin scrabbling around trailer parks in northern Montana, buying new trucks instead of paying the mortgage.

The moon was no more than a shank, and past the fire's glow all was darkness and the buzz of insects and the occasional motorboat out for a night cruise. Up to God knows what, but in my head it was always fornication. Everybody in the world fucking all the time, except me. Sara gathered her dress around herself. When she tugged it, it came off her shoulders. She gazed at the fire. I thought of taking off my shirt, giving it to her, and then taking it off her again. Her lips shone in the flickering light. What was she going to do with Carston, that ape? A whole lifetime trawling his hairy limbs. Till death, and he was the type who'd never die. Never leave you alone.

"And now you're getting married?" Hal said, straightening and seizing Carston's arm, his eyes suddenly bright. "Christ, the first of us." He hurled the vodka bottle toward the deck. It bounced off the side and landed spinning in the gravel. "Let's do it tonight. The last one here. My parents hitched right over there." He nodded down to where the dock had been.

Concern dampened Carston's high beams. "We already set a date. She's got her whole family coming up from Medford."

"You can still have that one. This'll just be for us, tonight. Old friends, the whole crew, at the cabin." Hal's voice was high with excitement and lies.

Sara watched, her face showing the look women get when they see the follies of men spread out before them. There's fear in it, and pity, too.

BEFORE I EVEN came to my senses, Hal had Cap and Till holding great flaming torches by the water and he was standing between them with a towel around his neck, hollering at everyone to get the fuck down here for the wedding. Jensen was next to him with his fist clamped shut and a triumphant gleam in his eyes that I'd seen for the first time when he was four and discovered how easy it was to pluck the legs from a spider.

There was nothing particularly clever or surprising about what happened next. As soon as Jensen opened his palm to reveal the two steel washers, and Hal started in about having and holding, I knew where the service was headed. Sara did, too, and even in the dark I could see the hurt in her eyes. Deep down, she must've known it since she pulled up and saw our mess of a crew, but she hadn't been ready to admit it.

We always want the world to be better than it is.

Not Carston, though. Standing under the torch with his chest out and his friends all around and his bride-to-be right across, he looked ready to start knocking down stars.

Jensen put one of the washers around the ring finger on Carston's left hand. Then he asked for Sara's. She tried to offer up her right, but he shook his head and Hal started to say something about ring fingers and she knew it was no use. She lifted the withered hand from her pocket and held it out, not slow, not shy, and I felt something inside myself sort of crumble. She was a proud kid, and in love.

Jensen leapt back like he'd been bit by a snake. His round snively face contorted into a grimace. Hal made a big show of trying to keep it together. He took the washer from Jensen and daintily poked it at the dangling helpless fingers before recoiling. The torchlight around them shook crazily as Cap laughed, and the whole thing degenerated when Cap doubled over, the flames at waist level, light licking Sara's upheld chin from below.

Till looked away, holding the torch in front of him. The Indians walked off down the shore toward the faint lights of Trego, the sledge swinging between their knees.

"I don't believe I can sanction this," Hal said, controlling himself for a moment. He closed his hand around the washer and drew it away. "Under God."

Carston made a grunting noise like a wounded animal. His wide eyes swung from Hal to Jensen. He was big enough that he could've stomped them both, done real damage, but it wasn't in him. Never had been. He lifted his trunk of an arm and let it fall. The steel went from his shoulders. He looked to me, as if I would make it right, but I was frozen and even enjoying his suffering in some deep and filthful part. As I always had.

The most he managed was to shake the washer free from his finger and fling it down into the dirt.

Sara put her hand away. She reached out with the other and pulled on Carston's arm. The silvery lake stretched out behind them, black mountain teeth above the far shore. She didn't look at me, at any of us. Carston's chin hung against his chest. His big forehead creased. He was stuck, confused, and fresh rounds of laughter ricocheted off the water.

I wanted to speak but my tongue was lead. Besides, what was there to say? There'd always be people like Hal and Jensen, and me. For whom anyone else's happiness was a spark to be snapped out, doused and trampled, for the light it threatened to hold to our own misery.

Sara kept tugging, and finally Carston moved. They made their way up between the blast craters on the hillside to his truck and climbed in. The engine roared to life. Brake lights glowed red. The doomed cabin loomed shoddily above the road, and down by the water the laughter began to fade. As I hoped the memory would, and so many of my other memories as well. I turned back to the fire—the hungry orange hearts at the base of each flame.

WAYS TO KILL A TREE

I WAS IMMEDIATELY AFRAID OF THE TREE. A LOOMING, decrepit pine nearly a hundred feet tall, it was like none of the others on the block. None of the others anywhere in the shabby suburb of Denver where my husband had brought us to live.

It looked like it belonged in a horror movie—all the shaggy branches dripping needles. Half the front yard was needle-covered dirt. No grass could grow in its shade. The pine smell was so thick I had to walk to the end of the block to get a breath of fresh air. All our neighbors had maples. A friendly line of them on the strip of grass between the side-walk and the street, their starry leaves going red.

I asked my husband to chop it down and he gave me one of the special twinkly smiles he saved for my foolishness. "We're renting," he said.

It was our first year of marriage and sometimes I wanted to set all of his belongings on fire. The carefully polished loafers he took off as soon as he came in the front door. The shelf of GMAT study guides. The flat-screen TV his mother had bought us, which he grunted at in a vaguely sexual way every time *SportsCenter* lit up the wide brilliant screen. His name was Dave. Somehow the full weight of this was just sinking in. *Dave*. I was Dave's wife, and when he unbuttoned the top button of his work shirt I had to keep from informing him how flabby his face was getting.

The tree stood perfectly straight, remarkably straight, and for all its shagginess it formed a long sharp arrowhead. I could see the tip piercing the sky when I pressed my face against our living room window. The cold of the glass traveled through my nose to my throat. I wondered why such meanness had come into my life.

After Dave went to work, I brought the ladder from the garage and climbed onto the roof. Scraping my knees on the rough shingles, I crawled to the peak and stood spread-legged, arms out, looking up. Wind made the upper branches tremble. I leaned forward, bracing myself in the October chill. I was wearing flip-flops. I was almost twenty-six and still only realized the dumb things I did when I was right in the middle of doing them.

A saw at the end of a long pole. A razor-sharp discus. I considered what other tools might be used to slice the tip off the tree. It would be a lot less threatening with a skuzzy little nub.

Ridiculous. I sat down, shivering, on the roof's peak. The house beneath me was a small sad box. Exactly what we could afford. It was a house, though. Complete with a bent little chimney and back door. No more studios and futons. No more mini-fridge full of condiments and take-out containers, a pint of half-melted ice cream wedged on a pizza in the icebox. We had a yard. We were practically adults.

Sunlight blasted my legs. Denver was always sunny and always cold. The roof peak dug into my butt. I rolled up the leg of my sweatpants and picked at the surgery scar on my knee. Then I looked down at the goose pimples on my bare calf. *What are you doing?* I wanted to cry, which made me even more angry, which made me even more sad. Wind gusted down the street and all the maples shook in unison like dogs. I thought of the places I'd rather be: deserts, beaches. Sunbathing beneath a palm in Santa Monica.

When Dave got home, I asked him, if I wanted to move, would we move.

"We just got here," he said, setting a bag with two burritos on the table.

"I know, I'm just saying if."

"We agreed. It's a good job, we're close to family, the mountains." I could see him growing tired as the months of discussion and lists of pros and cons came back. But we'd never talked about this tree. How had he not mentioned the tree?

"We're close to *your* family," I said.

"Your family is all over the place, and we can't afford L.A. We talked about this." He took a beer from the fridge, wedged the cap against the edge of the counter, and brought the flat of his hand down on it, popping the cap off and leaving a small chip on the counter's finish. The rented finish. His pale cheeks shook as he tipped his head back and drank. Wiping his mouth, he looked at me. "I mean, I need you to be happy."

"I don't think you're getting enough sunlight," I told him.

He sighed. "Is this about the tree?"

"No." I shook my head, glaring at the burritos. "We don't do anything here. I want to be people who do things."

"We went on a hike last weekend."

I shifted my eyes to stare at him. He was being paid $55,000 a year, plus benefits, to sell SAT preparation materials to school districts across the inner Northwest. Already he was settling into the job's shape and contours: long exasperated sighs, craft beers, khakis, a silver watch.

"We're going to get bikes. And tonight"—he set his beer down and slowly approached, swishing his hips inside his khakis—"I was planning to—"

"I feel sick," I said.

He grinned.

"I'm trying to talk to you. Can't you ever be serious?" The kitchen was too small—barely three feet between the stove and the opposite wall—and I hated the shrill tone in my voice. I took my emergency pack of cigarettes from the drawer, along with the stove lighter, and edged around Dave and out through the living room.

"Babe," he called after me.

The setting sun divided the yard into light and shadow. The grass on the unshaded half was stiff and turning brown. I crossed it, rapping the cigarette pack against my thigh. Growing up, my family had had a big, light-filled kitchen. A flyer for weed removal was speared to the top of the chain-link fence. I imagined a fire engulfing the tree. A lightning strike. *Crack*, and then dust. Even the roots burnt away. I rounded our car and stood in the road, looking down at my shadow stretching in front of me. A crazy elongated woman. I wasn't sure if I even wanted to be taken seriously.

The first stars peeked from the darkening sky around the tip of the tree. I clicked the long-necked stove lighter three times before it caught, then lit the cigarette and dragged in deeply. No cars passed. They hardly ever did on Weasley Street. It was toward the back of the development. To get out, you had to wind through the subdivision, along streets that had been renamed after Harry Potter characters, to the Red Robin by the freeway on-ramp. There were no black people here. One family of Mexicans. He'd cut me off from the world. I exhaled and watched the smoke travel up toward the stars.

Inside, Dave's shoulders were stooped over the kitchen table. He gazed down at his burrito, then leaned in for a bite. His head bobbed as he ate. I knew him better than I knew any other man on earth, but through the glowing window he was a stranger. He could've stood up, roared, and turned into a bear. Another family—wife, kids, golden retriever—could've come bounding up the stairs from the basement.

Then it would just be the tree and me in the yard, watching. Would I cry? Would it break my heart?

I hated the vast hazy sea of unknowing that surrounded my life.

Finishing the cigarette, I walked out of the road and stopped in front of the tree. "You," I said, stubbing the butt out on the trunk. Sparks showered the bark. None caught. I looked up into the branches. There were no squirrels, no birds. They knew better. I couldn't see to the top, it was so tangled. Had this been a forest once? An army of these monsters filling the valley, climbing the distant foothills. Maybe that's why this one was so pissed off. All its friends were gone and in their place were Dave and me.

He couldn't even wait for me to come back inside before he started to eat. "I don't want to be here, either," I said to the trunk.

A STORM RATTLED the windows late that night. I crawled out of bed, wrapped myself in a blanket, and went to the window. The tree's branches tossed and rolled, threatening to snap. Lightning split the sky. The branches leaned toward the house, groaning. In the right gust of wind, one could break off, smash through the window, and impale us to the bed.

"Dave," I said loudly.

He grunted and wrapped his arms around his pillow. When he slept, all the years fell off him and he looked like the little boy in the soccer uniform in the photos on his mom's fridge.

"It's storming," I said.

"Mmmm," he said. "It'll stop." He kissed the air where my shoulder would've been, and began to snore.

I got back in bed and lay awake for a long time, listening to him breathe and watching threads of moonlight waver between the branches.

WAYS TO KILL A TREE. I scrolled through the search results, surprised by how gleeful they were. Apparently people took pleasure in it, the same way you hear about puppy torturers and asphyxiating masturbators and all the other sickos. I saw pictures of slow deaths: small steady doses of pesticides, shallow incisions all the way around trunks. The withering.

Part of a branch was visible through the window. My hand grew clammy on the mouse. I told myself my interest was purely practical, a matter of survival, but my heart was pounding. The tree would suffer. More brutal sites featured custom-made saws and hatchets. Big horny spiked things that leather-vested men held on their shoulders in front of hacked-up mounds of wood and pulp.

I tried to picture Dave in one of the outfits and had to turn away from the computer, laughing. The sound filled the little office. He looked uncomfortable in shorts.

Pictures of us on our honeymoon in Argentina covered the bulletin board, my yoga mat leaned in the corner beside his record player. Wires were tangled atop the speakers; records piled inside cardboard boxes. Why hadn't we unpacked them? In Argentina, we'd waited for almost an hour in a line of tourists to kiss beneath a waterfall. I'd worn his T-shirts to bed. We'd listened to records. I'd been so in love I'd wanted to touch him all the time: at breakfast, on airplanes, in the grocery store. These things seemed unbelievable now. I felt completely alone.

The only woman I could find posted videos of herself plucking every leaf and bud from small saplings until they died. It struck me as depressingly, stereotypically feminine. Besides, it would take a thousand years to pluck every needle from that beast.

I was supposed to be looking for a job but I spent the rest of the day G-chatting with my college friends, reading about the dead idiot protesters in Oregon, looking up how many sexual partners the average woman has, and planning how, hypothetically, I'd kill the tree. It had to look natural. Inarguably natural, since Dave would suspect me. I decided some kind of insect was best. We'd call in the exterminator, he'd say, "Oh, an infestation," and the tree would have to come down. Our landlord would pay for the removal. Plus, I couldn't think of a worse fate than to be eaten to death by tiny insects you couldn't shake off.

Christ, I thought, clicking through Facebook. Am I a monster?

I'D MAJORED IN PSYCHOLOGY but I hadn't taken the premed courses that I needed to apply to grad school. My dad wanted me to go back and take them. Dave thought I should find a job, probably in digital marketing, like so many of my friends. "We have enough debt," he said. My marketing friends posted photos of themselves in short black dresses smiling hysterically in front of event backdrops. None of them were married, and when I went through their Coachella albums my toes started to curl, the nails digging into the hardwood floor.

It was surprisingly impossible to order invasive pine beetles online. I did, however, find a Japanese university professor who'd written a how-to guide on catching samples in the wild. I printed it out, then crumpled it up, threw it away, and brought the trash out to the can in the alley.

The next day, I went to the library. I could've kept researching online, but I tried to take an outing each day. It was one of the rules I'd made to keep myself from going crazy. Along with no daytime TV, no microwave meals, and yoga for at least twenty minutes every morning. I used the office. Scooting Dave's ergonomic desk chair into the hall and unrolling my mat, then twisting and swinging my arms and bending over into Dhanurasana, breathing deeply and trying not to feel like an idiot.

The bus picked me up four blocks from our house. Empty, save for an old man sleeping with his head on his arms. It hissed to a start and wound down Hermione Street into the traffic of Bear Valley, picking up passengers as we went. Burrs clung to the shoulder of the old man's army coat. I had to keep myself from crossing the aisle and plucking them off as the chain restaurants flickered past.

The library was a three-story brick building with a mismatched Grecian façade. Trying to tower, it squatted. The windows were tinted black and two dreadlocked bums, barely out of high school, sat on the steps with a banjo and a yellow lab.

"Hey, girl," one of them said.

"Hey, loser," I answered. But I didn't have a job, either. I smiled to myself, feeling young.

Inside, self-help books littered the FREE table by the door. I stood letting my eyes adjust to the dim light. Alarmed sensor gates flanked the entrance. The smell of old carpeting and mildewed pages was strong enough to make my eyes water. A poster of a bespectacled dachshund peering over the spine of *Madame Bovary* read TODAY'S READERS, TOMORROW'S LEADERS. Beyond the sensors, an obese young librarian was stamping books. Lifting the cover, she plunged the stamp down, snapped the cover shut, and slid the book to the left.

I patted my purse—making sure I hadn't somehow stolen anything—and passed through the sensors. I stopped in front of the librarian and leaned on the desk. She looked up. Her face was wide, rosy, and unwrinkled. The kind of skin that practically glows. Mounds of it. I felt sorry for her and jealous at the same time. "Can I help you?" she asked brightly.

"I'm looking for some information about pine trees." Her smile widened at the prospect—an eager young arborist.

Behind her, a cracked clock was struggling to keep up. I wrinkled my brow. "About . . . killing them."

Her smile disappeared, then with some effort reconstituted itself into concern. "Oh, you mean the beetles," she said. "It's so, so sad. We get lots of people asking about that." She shook her head. "They really are trying everything. The whole Environmental Studies Department at the U, Professor Worley in particular. She brings her classes out to Keystone Ridge to study them every semester. It's their little eggs, the beetles' little eggs that kills them, did you know that?" She shivered.

I stared at her, and she lifted a plump, equally rosy finger in the direction of the Environment section. "We have quite a collection. I can try to order anything you don't find."

A bearded man in a sleeveless yellow shirt was leaning his forehead against the end of the stack and chanting to himself. Homeless people were scattered throughout the library: sleeping in chairs, paging through magazines, urgently clicking at the bank of computers. They formed the majority of the clientele. I was about to follow her finger, when a sudden thought stopped me.

"Is there a place around here where I could see them? The beetles?"

"Oh, you haven't?" The librarian looked confused. "You must be new. Almost all the mountains near the city have patches. Most of the western slope of Mount Evans is just brown bones, and that's only since last year." Real sadness showed on her face. Maybe she'd lost her virginity there, caught up in the fervent arms of a clarinetist or speech-and-debater, gnarly roots scraping her butt.

"Is that . . . north?" I asked. There were mountains everywhere.

Her smile came back. "Just west of town. You take Highway 70 and get off in Idaho Springs. There's a marked Forest Service road up to the peak trail. You can't miss it."

I thanked her and walked past the bearded man. His eyes were closed, and his body formed a triangle with the shelf and the floor. He was chanting: *Elk. Elk, elk, elk,* like they'd done him wrong. Her job couldn't be easy.

Several of the environment books had chapters on mountain beetles. I took a small pile to the overstuffed orange chairs in the Children's section. Hanging cutouts of the Wild Things twisted slowly in the circulating air. A little girl perched on her knees and stared up at them. Her mother was slumped on a beanbag with an *Us Weekly* over her knee, her eyes slitted like a crocodile.

Motherhood. I dropped into the chair and sank deep in the cushion, feeling like a child myself with my knees above my stomach. According to the Internet, the median woman between the ages of twenty-five and forty-four has slept with four men. It seemed impossibly low; I'd heard my roommate go through twice that our freshman year. Shaking my head, I tried to concentrate on the books in my lap.

Death and Rebirth in the Age of Global Warming had a glossy insert in the center with pictures of great swaths of devastated forest paired up with statistics. Eighty-eight million acres had been destroyed in the western states and Canada—the number growing each year. The beetles were thriving in the shorter winters and hotter summers of the twenty-first century. They introduced fungus into the sapwood, preventing it from getting water and nutrients and bottling up the pitch flow, which usually repelled invading insects.

The pictures were terrible. Whole mountainsides brown and dry and dead. Fires raging. Smoke filling the sky. Sooty firemen leaning on axes looking athletically defeated.

I wondered how many I would need. Just two? A male and female? I imagined approaching the tree with a small Tupperware containing this Adam and Eve. Looking up at the scraggly menacing branches, the leaning trunk. Kneeling down over the roots and opening the lid. *Goodbye. Goodbye, goodbye, goodbye.*

I closed the book and looked at the little girl. Frowning, she pointed up at the largest cutout: a great woolly bull with human feet.

"I know," I said. "He's way up there."

DAVE BROUGHT BURRITOS home again that night. He liked to eat them at least twice a week. I'd cleaned the kitchen, really scrubbing the stove and fridge for the first time since we moved in. "Looks great," he said, plopping the bag on the counter. "Want to eat off the floor? Because we can."

Nimbly—I was always surprised by how nimble he was for his size—he nipped across the linoleum and kissed me on the forehead. I let him draw my cheek to his chest and stood there for a long moment listening to his heartbeat: *Dave, Dave, Dave.*

I wasn't sure if I was going to kill the tree, but the thought that I could made me feel better. I poured myself a glass of wine. Setting the table, Dave told me about a superintendent in one of his districts who was having an affair and how everyone used it to their advantage, but how he, Dave, wasn't sure he cared enough about selling flash cards and vocab booklets to do so.

"Who's he fucking?" I asked.

After dinner, we watched the news and then took a shower together. I didn't quite know how it happened. I said I was tired and the next thing I knew, Dave's big pink body was in the tub wrapped around mine, his right hand rubbing the small of my back in a way that made me feel both safe and nauseated. Water streamed through my hair. Soap and steam enveloped our limbs. His lips moved down my neck as if I were made of something so precious that a strong exhale might blow me away. *Squeeze my ass*, I wanted to say. *Slap me.* The bathroom's small window looked out at the side of the neighbor's house. Pressed against it, I could just make out the edge of the tree.

After, I opened the window and we toweled off as the steam faded from the mirror. "I need the car tomorrow," I said. "I'm going for a hike."

Dave tipped his head back and squinted into his nose in the mirror. "Okay. I'll bus to work." Fine blond hairs grew inside his nostril. He looked at me in the reflection. "I love you, Kat. You know that, right?"

I nodded, feeling aimlessly guilty. Part of me wanted to kiss the freckle on his pink shoulder. Another part wanted to run from the bathroom, down Weasley Street, and out of Denver, hopping into the back of the first truck that stopped.

MOUNT EVANS WAS BIGGER than any in Pennsylvania where I'd grown up, but it had the same craggy outcroppings of granite and indistinguishable clumps of brush. At first I couldn't see anything wrong. The trees were dense and green on both sides of the dirt road as I drove. Birds chirped. A hawk flew overhead. I wondered if the librarian, like most of the large women I'd known, was prone to exaggeration.

Then suddenly, as if someone had flipped off a light switch, every tree was dead. Every branch, every twig, every needle: brown and desiccated. And with them went the sounds of the forest. All I heard was the car's grumbling engine, the tires bouncing over ruts in the road. Bubbles of dried sap marked wounds on each brown trunk. Scores of them, hundreds. They were like the sores on plague victims and every time I focused on one I had to look away. I drove for another mile into this wasteland, then pulled off and got out.

The cool fall air was thick with the smell of decaying wood. I adjusted the brace on my knee, then walked up off the road, picking through the underbrush to a large pile of boulders. Each one was the size of our car. I scrambled up the sides, my knee aching. I could remember the pop it made when the meniscus tore, and how I could never play soccer as well again, but I couldn't remember the pain. "That's how childbirth will be," Dave had said, before we were even engaged.

I paused, leaning my cheek against the rock. It was cool and soundless but possessed a vibration, a deep note. If I listened long enough I'd hear something. Dave had always been so sure. That was his gift. But what about me, out here on this mountain? Hunting beetles, going to war with a tree?

I touched my stomach, trying to imagine it swelling, a tiny helpless person forming inside. *What do you want?* I'd say to her, or him, for eighteen years. *I love you, what do you want?* I pushed myself up and kept climbing.

At the top of the rocks, I straightened on the pebbly ledge and looked out across the slope. A brown sea stretched in all directions. For miles and miles. Along the edges, a battle was being waged. Pockets of green clinging to life between the extending brown fingers. I'd read that the part of the tree you see is only the upper half; the taproot stretches down as deep as the crown is high. I imagined this under-forest in the black dirt and bedrock, unable to understand what had happened above. I shivered. The horizon was washed out, gray. It looked like the world was about to end. Where had Dave brought me? At least on the East Coast you could always hear a car.

I searched the near trunks and even though I couldn't see the beetles, I could imagine them from the pictures in the books—their black armored backs and eyeless faces. Squirming beneath the bark. No bigger than a grain of rice with spiky jointed legs. Thousands, millions of them, coring out the wood, excreting their fungus. Gorging themselves and mating and then moving on, insatiable, to the next.

UMPQUA

EVERY FEW MILES, REFLECTIVE SIGNS MARKED THE NORTH Umpqua Trail. Bun read each of them in a high singsong voice: *North Umpqua Trail Swiftwater, North Umpqua Trail Mott Creek.* It gave her small pleasure to irritate me, and on other nights it had given me small pleasure, too.

"Shut up," I said.

She turned to the window. Hundred-foot Doug firs loomed above the highway; the lights of Glide were far behind us.

"Isn't it enough I have to listen to you at home?"

"When do you ever listen to me at home?"

"Christ."

"Can I breathe?" she asked. "Can I move my arms?"

The tallest Doug firs were black spears against the sky,

which was the final darkest shade of blue, and just beginning to be punctured by stars. I toed down the accelerator. I could feel Bun's eyes on the side of my face.

"You're depressed and you want everyone else to be depressed, too," she said. "I don't know why I came." Her bleached ponytail caught flashes of passing headlights. She shifted her hips toward the door, as if she were going to step out at sixty-five miles per hour. I had a vision of her big body tumbling down the pavement.

"He was my friend," I said.

"I never met him."

"Yes, you did."

Bun shrugged, looking out the window. "I didn't recognize him on the news." A semi with its brights on roared past. I squinted at the stars over the steering wheel. My dad used to tell me they were God shooting holes in the sky, back when I'd believe anything.

"He was at the party after Tony's wedding."

"I met about a thousand people that night," she said. "I met most of Douglas County. You never talked about him."

"We were close when we were kids, and then in high school."

"At Sutherlin?"

I nodded.

"Who were his parents?"

"I told you he was my friend. Isn't that enough, for Christ's sake?"

We passed the final sign for the North Umpqua Trail and I turned off the highway onto the Toketee Lake road. I listened to Bun breathe in the passenger seat. I could tell she was counting to five in her head with each exhale.

"He and I used to come up here together," I said.

She turned to the trees and flicked a piece of dirt off her long pink nail. "It's going to be crowded."

"Not on a Monday night."

"It's spring break. All the schools are out."

The muscles in my jaw tightened.

"You didn't know that?"

"Why would I know that?"

"Most people know," she said. Ahead, the half-moon rose over Diamond Peak. The pavement ended. We bumped over potholes. Wedges of Toketee Lake shone through the Doug fir branches. The still water glittered like oil. Lonnie wasn't the first person I'd known who got shot: a girl from my middle school was in the class at UCC when Christopher Harper-Mercer came through with his Glock, but I'd never really talked to her. She was just a face to me. Lonnie was my closest friend in middle and high school, until he dropped out. A single dark Winnebago was parked in the closed campground. It was far too late to turn back.

"You like it when I'm mad," I said. "You enjoy it."

Bun turned to me, held my eyes for a moment, and then shook her head. It was a look I'd been getting for years. As if she'd opened me up and didn't like what she saw inside.

THE DIRT LOT at the trailhead was full, and more cars were parked along the dirt road. I swung around and pulled in behind a minivan. It had Olympic National Park and Rainbow Gathering stickers on the bumper, and one that read UNFUCK THE WORLD on the back window. Hippies were always coming down to the hot springs from Eugene. Balancing rocks, whittling. Shit that only hippies have time to do. I'd hoped the violence around Little Charbonneau and along the borders of the Redoubt would scare them off, but nobody worried about anything unless it was right in front of them. I cut the engine, sat back, and let the dark settle in around us. Bun was silent. Her figure seemed to grow and loom over me as the Doug firs had. I wanted to reach across the cupholder and squeeze her thigh, as if that might shrink her down to size.

"You going to change here?" I asked.

"I left my suit at home."

"You did what?"

"I left it at home."

"What'd you think we were coming out here for?"

"Maybe just to fight," she said.

I gripped the steering wheel. With the heat off, the air in the car was turning cold.

"It'll be dark anyway," she said.

"Anyway?" I pictured the college kids watching her take off her clothes. Not laughing outright, saving it for later, on the ride back to Corvallis. My face grew hot. "You can wear a T-shirt."

"I don't want to wear a T-shirt."

Her door creaked loudly, the rending sound of metal on metal. It hadn't opened right since my brother T-boned me coming out of our driveway in high school. Cold air rushed in. Bun stepped out, shivered, and stretched her back. Then she leaned into the backseat for a towel.

"I don't like it," I said. "You know I don't like it."

She brushed a strand of hair out of her face and glared at me. Parts of her, like the lobes of her ears, were so delicate they hurt me to look at. "What *do* you like?"

"All kinds of things, just not a bunch of hippies and old men staring at you with their dicks out."

She pulled a pink towel from the wad of dirty clothes in the backseat. "Nobody else will be wearing a suit. It's embarrassing."

"This is embarrassing. This is embarrassing for me."

"Well, you can stay in the fucking car." Bun straightened, slung the towel over her shoulder, slammed the door with another horrible sound, and walked down the road toward the trailhead.

I rolled the window down, cranking as hard and fast as I could. "Yeah? You can find another ride home." I paused. "He was my *friend*."

Her figure disappeared behind the outhouse. I sat in the dark. I knew I was going after her, I had been for years. The thought of her with anyone else made my stomach feel like it was sliding down through my intestines. Lonnie hadn't had a girlfriend, or wife. Maybe that was why it was so easy for him to leave.

A misty rain began to fall as soon as I got out of the car. I walked around the back and opened the trunk. The cooler had leaked on the clothes strewn across the upholstery. Staring down at the soppy mess was almost funny, and then I wondered if Lonnie had regretted what he'd done, in the instant before the first bullet ripped through his chest.

"YOU REMEMBER WHAT happened to Cami Springer?" I asked, when I caught up with Bun on the footbridge over the Umpqua River. The sound of the water, loud as a revved motor, swallowed my words. She kept walking and I thought she might not have heard. "You remember—"

She stopped and turned. Her eyes flashed above her round cheeks. "Of course I remember."

My mouth went dry. "I'm trying to look out for you."

"Look out for me? Look out for me by bringing up Cami Springer? That was in high school. At a keg."

"That was at night, in the woods, skinny-dipping."

"What's wrong with you?"

The beam of a headlamp swung toward us. A flannel-shirted couple were sharing a rotisserie chicken on the rear bumper of a van in the parking lot. Preppy kids on a road trip, taking pictures in front of waterfalls. I wondered if they could see the disgust on Bun's face. I kicked away a Doug fir needle from between my toes and raised my middle finger. The beam swung back across the lot.

"I'm not going to listen to you," she said. "Not tonight. Not anymore." She swiped her forearm across her eyes, turned, and walked over the bridge. Her dirty pink windbreaker swished with each step.

"That's great," I called after her. "That's perfect." I hefted the cooler and followed; the beer cans clunked against each other. There couldn't possibly be enough inside.

The path began to climb steeply on the far shore. Bun swayed from side to side, clutching the wood handrail for support. In a hundred yards, the path forked. The left fork went three miles back to Toketee Lake, where it connected to the rest of the North Umpqua Trail. The hot springs were a quarter mile up to the right. I paused, remembering hiking in with Lonnie in high school. Talking about what types of girls we'd see, then staying for hours in the pools with the steam and bodies until it got to be too much and I thought I might explode up over the river and travel in a ball of fire all the way back to Sutherlin.

A campfire glowed on the opposite shore. It could've been Umpqua Indians come back to life. Painted like warriors, wondering what to do about all these college kids at their springs. I stepped off the path to let two scrawny teenagers pass. Net shorts clung to their legs. The second one nodded to me with his pimply chin. I made a gun with my thumb and forefinger and shot him in the side of the head.

Boy howdy, Lonnie used to say.

Bun stopped at the top of the cliff and leaned against the handrail. Her cheeks were flushed. She sucked in air. She looked down at the rushing water, eyes shining. "You used to be proud to take me places," she said. "Do you remember that? How we'd drive to Roseburg for dinner?"

"Maybe we'll get our own pool," I said.

It wasn't impossible. One of the lukewarm ones down by the river. She could be as naked as she wanted then, her big wet tits like buoys. The first time I saw them—at halftime of a Bulldogs game in the back of her sister's car—I'd thought everything was going to be all right, that I'd finally found my place in the world. I leaned over the rail. The half-moon cast an icy reflection on the rapids a hundred and fifty feet below. I imagined jumping off. Plummeting through the air. I didn't exactly think I'd die at the bottom, that was the funny part. I wanted to see what would happen.

Bun caught her breath and pushed off the handrail. Her flushed cheeks glowed. She held her arms out at her sides, as if she didn't want them to touch her stomach.

I switched the cooler to my right arm. "Will you just wear a T-shirt, please?"

A WOOD SHELTER covered the main pool. The smell of weed drifted out. Purple and blue towels hung from the rails. Inside, a man was talking loudly about his dog killing a squirrel. "I fried up the heart," he said. "Wasn't bigger than a walnut, but me and Smoky shared it. Was her first kill."

The two other pools up top were full of dark, long-haired heads. One of the groups had brought a pit bull into the water with them. It sat unmoving in the center, mouth open, probably about to have a heart attack from the heat.

"Let's check down below," I said.

But Bun was already moving into the shelter. "Those aren't hot enough."

I set the cooler down in the mud and used my towel to wipe the rain from my forehead. "Goddammit." The sky was black now and stars shone between the clouds. I rubbed my aching shoulder. The sound of many low voices created a buzz in the air. A black-haired girl moved onto the rocks on the edge of the near pool. She leaned back, looked up at the sky, and let the rain fall on her bare breasts.

"Cassiopeia," she said.

The man beside her tipped his head back. His uncircumcised dick floated on the moonlit water. "Maybe," he said.

I picked up the cooler and went after Bun.

A lighter sparked over a bowl when I stepped onto the shelter's deck. Four faces shone in the flickering orange light: Smoky's owner, a leathery old hippie with a dripping beard and scarred cheek who I thought I'd seen there years before, a young couple, probably nineteen, sitting in the corner, the girl leaning against the boy's chest, the boy with his arm around her shoulders, her nipples just hidden by the water, and a fat teenager who looked too stoned to move. Bun was in the far corner unzipping her coat. I put the cooler down and took out a beer.

"Nice night," I said.

"Goddamn nice night." The hippie lifted the bowl in salute. The scar ended in a pucker by his lips. Flesh below it was drawn in against the bone, as if some were still missing. It didn't make him look tough so much as crumpled. "Goddamn nice every night up here."

The couple smiled and nodded. The teenager didn't even flinch. If he slid down a couple more inches, I figured he'd drown. Another empty seat in remedial math. The weed smoke and steam made me light-headed. Bun hung her coat over the rail. All she had on underneath was a white undershirt. Her bare arms were pink and soft and my heart began to pound.

"They've got a dog in the pool up there," I said.

"Hey, Smoky!" the hippie called. He waited a moment, then, hearing nothing, went on. "It's not her. She doesn't even like coming near the pools. Too hot." He set the bowl and lighter down and pushed his greasy hair back. "We do most everything else together. Been living down the way for the past couple months."

The boy from the couple turned to him. "Were you here when they found the body?" he asked.

I stared, wondering how they knew about Lonnie, before realizing, of course, they were talking about someone else.

The hippie nodded slowly. "Sure wish I hadn't been."

"They said he just passed out, went under."

"Guess you could call it that. He was a drunk. Must've been seventy-five but he came up here most nights. Hiked in around midnight, then stayed in the pool drinking. Finally his heart couldn't take it."

Bun was unbuttoning her pants. I went and stood behind her. People died in the pools every couple years. Bums or teenagers who got too wasted. Her rounded shoulders were like snowy hills. "You ready for a beer?" I asked.

"Sure."

I leaned into her ear and lowered my voice. "I don't care if this T-shirt gets wet, it's an old one."

Her shoulders stiffened. "*Russel.*"

I squinted down at her earlobe. Plump and pink with two silver studs. I wanted to take it between my teeth and pull her out of the shelter like a wolf pup. Pull her all the way home. I took a drink. I could feel six eyes watching me. "Then don't ask me for anything else," I said.

She shook her head quickly. Like a fool, I backed off toward the cooler. I stood there out of the steam and watched the black-haired girl gaze up at the stars. A drop of water clung to the tip of her nose, hanging on for all it was worth. I thought of licking up her chest and sucking it off. I thought of how it felt to turn a gun toward yourself, even just a little bit. Okay. I pulled my shirt over my head and tightened the drawstring on my orange swim trunks. Fine. I walked back into the shelter.

Bun had her jeans halfway down her thighs, revealing a sagging pair of teal panties. Her head was tilted as she unclasped her earrings. She never did things in the right order. She paused when she saw me, then set the earrings on the rail, bent, and pushed the jeans all the way down to her ankles. The panties had lace frills along the band. I'd gotten them for her. I swatted a mosquito from my neck.

"Out early this year," the hippie said.

I looked over. I thought I might swat him next.

Bun hung the jeans by her earrings, then pulled her undershirt over her head. Fat hung loose on her pale sides. It was dented with patterned marks from the seat of my car. Her skin was so soft that even the lightest touch left a mark. Like a bun in the oven. I caught the boy from the couple looking at her around his girlfriend's shoulder. Bun had beautiful skin. I always thought that, even if there was too much of it. She draped the undershirt over her jeans, and without hesitating slid the teal panties down and off her feet. She left them there crumpled on the deck, looking helpless. My heart thudded.

Her heavy breasts rested on her stomach, her stomach hung over her groin, the whole length and breadth of her in the dim light. She was so much more naked out here than in our bedroom. The tucked-away curls of her pubic hair made me feel like I was running out of air.

She stepped calmly to the edge of the pool. The surface of the water looked taut in the moonlight, like shards of glass. Bun held her hands over her breasts and slowly lowered herself in. Tiny bubbles rose around her arms. "Ah," she said. "That's better."

I listened to my heart in my ears and thought about the Indians—how now would be a good time for them to come war-whooping in.

———

AN HOUR AND FOUR BEERS LATER, we were joined by a pair of baseball players from OSU who'd hiked in on the North Umpqua Trail all the way from Glide—fifty miles over three days—and the conversation turned back to the old drunk.

"It doesn't sound too bad," the bigger of the two said, sitting with his arms outspread, the cocksure posture of a lifelong jock. A towel-snapper, the kind who put their balls on each other in the locker room. "They say freezing to death is best, but I could think of a lot worse ways than passing out in a hot pool and not waking up."

"Like getting shot?" I asked. Bun's eyes blinked open. She hadn't moved since getting in. Had sat there, three inches away, like a dormant sea creature, and not looked at me once. But I had her attention now. "A friend of mine got shot dead yesterday. We used to come up here together."

All the eyes around the pool turned to me. "At Little Charbonneau?" the boy said, a hushed tension in his voice. His girlfriend raised her head from where it had been nuzzled into his neck. How long had they been together? A few months? Everything was easy at first. Bun and I used to squeeze into the special double seat in the movie theater just so we could be touching the whole time.

I nodded. "Took seven feds with them."

"They've got camps all over Harney County, and Lake, too, from what I hear," the hippie said.

"That's where it started."

"It's crazy." The boy looked at me. "What do they even want?"

"Their land," I said. "*Our* land. For the government to start minding the Constitution, instead of murdering patriots."

"Russ, please," Bun said quietly.

"People are fed up. We're losing our rights. We've already lost them."

"So then what?" the baseball player said. "They go out to the middle of nowhere and take over a bird refuge and shoot some cops?"

"They shot first."

They were all staring at me.

"Then the rest of the country. Get it back from the criminals who've run it into the ground."

The boy's girlfriend touched his arm. "I'm getting hot," she said, and rose from the water. Her body was slim and gawky, not yet fully grown, with large puffy nipples. She reached for her towel. "Hon?" The boy didn't move. His eyes were locked on mine across the water. I wondered what he was majoring in: painting, maybe, or environmental studies. What firm his father worked for.

Slowly, he stood.

"That's how everything starts," I said. "People finally have enough."

The boy opened his mouth but his girlfriend shook her head rapidly, and he followed her, wrapping himself in a towel and disappearing into the darkness. The half-moon shone down on the inky treetops on Mowich Ridge.

"Better go and see about my dog," the hippie said.

AFTER THEY WERE GONE, Bun scooted around to where they'd been sitting, leaving me alone on the far side of the pool. She changed the subject, asking the baseball players about the hike in, how long it took, where they'd camped. They kept looking at me as they answered. The stoned kid drowsed on, oblivious. Drops glistened on the curve of Bun's throat. Her flushed skin was rosy, like her whole body was blushing. Every time I thought I was ready to never see her again, I saw something like that. I opened another beer. It had to be almost midnight. The steam and the rails made it hard to see the other pools. If Lonnie had been there, we'd have done a lap. Started at the very bottom pool, maybe even dunked in the river to cool off, then gone in each of the six on the way up, seeing what there was to see.

I drank again. My head was foggy, plagued by an anger I couldn't straighten. Lonnie didn't have to worry about his anymore. That was one thing you could say for him. I lifted my hand and looked at the pruny fingers, each digit notched and bent, born into this mess. Years of pumping gas, loading trucks. I tried to imagine what it would be like to join up. Squatting in a tent under the butte, listening to the FBI drones overhead. Eating camp rations. At least I'd be doing something. I'd heard there were whole towns in the Redoubt like that: people standing up for themselves, not taking any more shit.

I looked at the stars. "What time is it? I've got work tomorrow."

Bun didn't turn. I could tell she wanted to pretend she hadn't heard. "Just a little longer," she said.

The bigger baseball player smirked. "Work? What're you worrying about work for? Aren't you quitting and joining the revolution, with the rest of the welfare cowboys?"

I squinted into the steam. He had twenty pounds on me at least, and a friend. "Lots of times I wonder why people open their mouths at all," I said.

"That's cute."

"What do you know?"

"I know there are people in the world who are really suffering. Who've got real things to worry about, like getting enough to eat. Not some idiot rednecks trashing state parks and murdering people."

The tops of the Doug firs swayed in the moonlight. "Russ," Bun said. Eye shadow had leaked around her eyes like she'd been crying, but she hadn't been. She didn't even care that my friend was dead, or that our country was going to hell, or that this cocksucker was talking down to me.

"I bet you've never worked a day in your life." I leaned forward. The stoned kid rose and slunk off into the darkness, leaving a gleaming trail of drips behind him.

The baseball player shifted. Straightening and bringing his

arms together. "I work, summers for my dad's construction company."

"*Summers* for my *dad*."

He set his jaw. "Because I'm in college," he said. "You belong in jail. Every one of you. The only thing wrong with this country is you."

I thought if I pushed off the rocks and lunged at him, I might crack his nose before he got a punch in, but who knew what his friend would do. I'd never fought two naked men in a hot pool before.

"Jesus Christ," Bun said. "Stop it. Please, I came here to relax."

The fear in her voice drew a deep, suffocating sadness over my anger. Her lips were bloodless, her makeup ruined. I blew out the breath I'd been holding and looked up at the moon. A half-shut eye, not much use. "Fine," I said.

I stood up. The hot water poured off me and the shock of cold air set in. "Stay. With these fucks. I'm leaving."

I dried off as quick as I could, rubbing my chest and head, then my legs and feet, all the feeling returning in prickly bursts. The baseball players watched silently, judgment written across their faces. Working summers for my dad would've meant sitting around drinking and waiting for the old paper mill to reopen. Waiting forever. Bun's lips parted, but she didn't say a word. Misty clouds clung to the treetops. I slid on my flip-flops and grabbed the cooler. "Good luck finding a ride."

"Don't get yourself killed, now," the baseball player said. "Like your friend."

I picked my way as fast as I could across the wet rocks, yellowish from sulfur. The pit bull was gone and the Cassiopeia girl was gone. My overheated legs wobbled. A few heads turned to watch. I thought about cursing them. Telling them exactly what I thought. Channels funneled the hot water down from one pool to the next. You could drop a tennis ball in and watch it go all the way down. The first time I'd seen it, I'd wondered who could've engineered such a thing. Now I knew it was just a bunch of perverted old hippies.

I found the path and plunged down the side of the cliff, sliding on the cold mud, catching myself on the handrail, nearly running. The rain had stopped and the sky was riddled with stars. "Fuck you, Bun," I said. Staying up there, to *relax*. Leaving me to come down all alone. Lonnie leaving me, too, and the world, for that matter. My head was so muddled and hot I thought it might burn out like a fuse.

The Umpqua River was louder than ever. I crossed the footbridge, banging the cooler against my thigh, getting madder with every step. The whole country pressed in on the dark trees around me—Portland and Seattle, self-driving cars, smart watches, robots—trying to push me out. Like I wasn't good enough to be here anymore. Like I was something to be ashamed of, as if we hadn't built it in the first place.

Bun could drown up there with them, like the old drunk had, for all I cared.

I skirted the outhouse and clambered up to the road. The

Pontiac gleamed dully in the moonlight. It was the only car I'd
ever owned: a manta-green Grand Am. I bought it used in high
school with money I'd saved pumping gas. I unlocked the door
and tossed the cooler into the backseat. The top flew off and beer
and ice spilled across the floor. I leaned in and grabbed a beer and
a handful of ice. Then I slammed the door, ate the ice, and walked
around to the driver's side. I thought about the shitty trailer Bun
and I shared. The sink full of dishes, crumbs scattered across the
living room table, water stains on the sagging ceiling. I opened
the can and took a long drink. It tasted metallic, sour, but it woke
me up. I got in the car and turned the key.

The engine choked, hacked, caught. I could drive straight
out to the Redoubt. Why not? I flipped on the brights and spun
the wheels so they shrieked. Bun. That was why. Who knew
what she'd do if I left her here with those baseball players.
Dirt shot back into the road. I jammed the gas and peeled out,
then flipped a hard right into the parking lot. Two vans and
a truck were parked at the far end. Rich kids, hippies. I spun
around, not slowing down. Mud spewed from the squealing
tires. I looped, then jammed the gas again. Coming in harder,
spinning donuts, like in high school. The V6 roared. I hoped
she could hear.

A light came on in one of the vans. "Shut the fuck up!" a
man yelled.

So they were trying to sleep. It made me even madder. I
rolled the window down and spun again, harder. I remembered the hill over French Pond, looking down at Cami
Springer naked on the little sand beach, five or six guys gath-

ered around her. Me and Lonnie and some others just standing on the hill, watching. The Pontiac's back tire jumped over a rock. I heard a chunking sound. I thought about how I used to polish my boots before taking Bun to the Applebee's in Rose- burg, the pink heart earrings she wore. I hit the accelerator. She had to hear. The trunk bounced off a stump. I spun again and the whole car leapt forward. I realized I was redlining it, but I couldn't make myself stop.

Big ridged circles chewed the lot. I drove the gas to the floor, shot forward, bounced, and yanked the wheel as far to the left as it would go. I saw Bun's naked body rising from the water, glowing, swelling, blocking out the horizon, a look in her eyes like she was going to pass right through. I saw the baseball players with their shit-smirking grins and college futures. Becoming bosses, becoming the boss's bosses. The front wheels turned but the momentum was too much and the rear tires skidded out. The bumper flew off the embankment, slammed down, and crashed into a tree. My head snapped for- ward, then back, and everything was quiet save for the roar of the river and the tick of the dying motor.

A whining noise filled my ears. My head hurt. I fumbled around for my beer but it had flown back into the rear win- dow. A drop of blood ran down my bare chest. I realized I'd left my T-shirt at the pools. It made me want to cry. I touched my bleeding nose and pain shot up my forehead. "No, no, no," I mumbled. I pushed open the door and pitched out into the loose earth and ferns.

Half crawling up the embankment, mumbling curses, I

pulled upright at the top. My head pounded. I was covered in mud. I looked down at the wreck of my car.

The hood was angled up toward the moon as if it were about to take off. The smashed bumper was folded around a huge Doug fir trunk. Smoke rose from the engine. The smell of burnt rubber stung my nose. The first time I'd seen it, parked in front of Gold and Silver Exchange, freshly waxed and shining with the price written across the windshield, I'd thought it was the most beautiful thing in the world. Misty, I'd called her. Misty June. Now I had no way of getting home. No way of getting anywhere.

Who'd even want me if I tried to join up? I'd probably shoot my own ass off.

Flashlights appeared high on the path across the river. They were moving fast, the beams bouncing wildly. I looked around as if I might run or hide. I thought if anyone got out of one of the parked vans and said a single word I'd hurl myself into the river.

Bun came down first, running and stumbling. She paused at the bottom and squinted in my direction. Then she rushed across the footbridge, her whole body moving in a rolling run. Her clothes were thrown on, her jacket unzipped. She stopped at the edge of the lot by the outhouse. She stared at the wreck, then at me. Her chest heaved. Her face was pale, with bright red blooms on each cheek. Beautiful.

"Oh, Russ," she said.

"Look." I lifted my arm, my pointing finger shaking. "Look what you did to my car."

STAY HERE

I

Whoever it was that hurt you, let me hurt them

DARKNESS HAD BEGUN TO FALL BY THE TIME WE REACHED Onekama. Kimia slowed the rental car—a bright red Chevy Volt that seemed to be made entirely of plastic—and peered out the window. The look in her brown eyes was as if she'd forgotten if this was the right place. We could have been anywhere. I imagined her running across a wide empty field toward a precipitous edge that I could not see. Shadows cloaked the buildings. A hardware store, a restaurant. Empty lots filled with weeds. Three deer looked up to watch us pass. The still water of Portage Lake shone behind them. It was my first time in Michigan, and though I had not yet spoken to another person, I felt exposed. As I did when Kimia visited my family in Montana. Her ethnicity a question, a hesitation, to be prodded and wondered at with bright, figuring eyes. "But you grew up here? Your English is amazing." When her family had been in this country for nearly a hundred years.

"That used to be a bar." Kimia nodded at a red storefront with plywood over the windows. "They had chicken strips." Her features softened. The setting sun glinted off her large turquoise rings. She had always spoken of this town, and her family's cabin here, in a way that made me suspicious. As if it were a perfect place where nothing bad ever happened, when so much bad had happened in her childhood. One long summer's day, running down sand dunes hand in hand with her sister while their parents watched from a blanket in the shade. Stealing booze from liquor cabinets, swimsuits left crumpled on the dock. If I thought about it too hard my head would start to ache.

We continued on for another half mile, past a public park with a boat ramp, a blue-steepled church. More deer grazed in the churchyard. Houses were set far apart along the road, some bigger, some smaller, all modest. Factory workers whose families had pooled their savings for a weekend place. We rounded a bend and Kimia drew in her breath. I followed her eyes to a small white structure on the narrowing strip of land between the road and the lake. It was not at all what I had expected, or thought of as a cabin. Just a house. A single-story box with a shingle roof and metal trim, white paint flaking off the walls. A large pipe ran up from the electric meter through the eaves to a tangle of power lines.

"Ben Raafat," Kimia said softly, reading the wooden sign hanging next to the meter, her great-grandfather's name. We had been in the car for almost fourteen hours. New York, Pennsylvania, Ohio, and now Michigan. She slowed and bumped over the shoulder onto the grass. There was no driveway. She parked in a patch of dirt by the side door. An old gnarled white pine, the only tree in the yard, loomed over the windshield. Kimia smiled tiredly. She turned to the cabin, and I think she was surprised by how small and run-down it was, too. A decade had gone by since she had last been. I reached across the cupholder and squeezed her thigh.

"I hope I can find the key," she said.

It was supposedly hidden where it had always been: on a nail in the crawl space below the floor. Kimia dragged away the warped piece of plywood by the front stoop and we stared down into the darkness of the concrete trench. Spiders scuttled from view. Wood lattice hung nearly to the ground. Webs strong enough to snare rodents were spun diagonally from the lattice to the dirt. Indistinguishable bits of trash littered the edges, along with a length of rusted pipe. Kimia sighed, and stepped down inside. The setting sun cast an amber light that stretched my shadow nearly across the road. She adjusted the blue bandanna she wore to hide her black hair—it was an odd length that summer, in the midst of growing out, and it embarrassed her, though I liked it—and knelt. She used the pipe to clear away the worst of the webs. Then she reached under the lattice into the pure dark of the crawl space and felt around for the nail. Her eyebrows drew together in concentration.

"You sure it's there?" I asked.

A large pickup rumbled past. The driver was the first other person I had seen since arriving in Onekama. Round, red-faced, and surly, he stared at me from beneath the low bill of his Cummins baseball cap. There was something threatening in his gaze, like a scout from an opposing army. The violence in the Redoubt had made me suspicious of men in trucks, men who looked like those I had grown up with. When he noticed Kimia's head in the trench, his eyes widened. She nodded, determined. She lay down on her back and squeezed her body under the lattice. More spiders scurried forth. I had the disturbing sense, not for the first time, that she was capable in a way I was not. That she had been tested and come out stronger than I would ever be. I waited in the grass, looking around, hoping no one else would pass and see her wriggling beneath the house, only her skinny jeans and brown boots showing, as if she were trying to escape.

"Found it!" she called, her voice muffled.

AN AGGRESSIVE, ROTTEN, FECAL SMELL greeted us when she opened the door. "Jesus." I raised my arm over my nose, and bumped the two suitcases over the doorsill. Abandoning them in the entryway, I peered into the kitchen sink, then joined Kimia in the bathroom. Brown liquid filled the toilet nearly to the brim. It had a murky depth and texture, like a horrible cauldron, the underside of the world. Irregular white patches of mold floated on top.

"I don't think anyone's been here since last summer. It must have come back up." The flush handle clanked uselessly when Kimia pressed it. She bit her upper lip. Dirt streaked her shirt. The expression of forced calm on her face threatened to break. She hardly ever cried, ever, but now I was afraid she might. We were faced with a year's worth of standing shit. We were supposed to sleep in the next room. The plunger looked laughable. I thought of hotels. I thought of driving back to New York. We would not arrive until the next morning, in the swell of rush-hour traffic.

Kimia called her mom as I walked through the cabin opening windows. The interior was an open L-shape around an enclosed bedroom. It took less than a minute to see the whole thing. The smell was least repugnant in the far front corner. I stood there by the large window facing the lake. I pressed my nose against the screen and inhaled, desperate for a scent of fresh moving water. The last light glowed violet on the horizon. The far shore was a low, snakelike silhouette, slithering toward where it broke apart and Portage Lake emptied into the much larger waters of Lake Michigan. I thought of the droplets flowing toward that expanse. Did they know of waves? I felt unsettled. Stuck and vaguely afraid, as if I were somewhere I should not be.

You're tired, I told myself.

By the time I finished bringing in the rest of our luggage, Kimia was off the phone. I heard a flush. "It was the power," she said, meeting me in the kitchen, her face shining with relief. "I just had to flip the breakers."

"Breakers." I shook my head, as if they had been the source of much misery in my life. I reached out and tucked her bandanna back over her forehead. She stepped into my chest and wrapped her arms around my waist. I set my chin on her head, smelling the argan-oil freshness of her hair.

"I'm glad you're here," she said.

THE MONTH BEFORE, I had opened Kimia's phone and seen a strange message from her sister. *I miss your body so much.*

I stared down at the screen, trying to make sense of the words. My stomach went cold, and what felt like a cold eel twisted inside it. She and her sister were close, but this? The whole time? It made me think I would never really know anyone at all. I could barely read the rest of the conversation, my heart was pounding so hard: more about Kimia's body, how beautiful it was, how hard to live without. Her responses were measured but encouraging. She, too, missed this touch, this nearness. And then suddenly came a photo of a completely naked man, his right hand raised to hold his phone, his body captured in the sickly reflection of what appeared to be a public restroom mirror. Looking closer, I saw that the muscles in his chest were flexed, and that his penis was a much darker color than the rest of his skin. Oddly, it matched the red detailing on the far tile wall.

How could this be?

My brain clicked into function and I recognized him: her ex-boyfriend, from Buffalo. She had saved his number under her sister's name to hide it from me. They had been together for seven years before we met. He worked for his father, some kind of inland shipping magnate. Steel, beams, things with one syllable. He had asked her to marry him. My relief turned to a slowly dawning anger. Was this better than incest? I scrolled further back. Near the beginning of the conversation, I found a picture of Kimia. It was one she had also sent me, except the version she sent him was cropped just below her bare shoulders, while the one in my phone showed her breasts and the whole upper half of her body. I stared at the cropped photo. It represented some boundary on her part, some prudence, *if he can't see my tits* . . . but she had miscalculated. The cropped photo was more intimate. Her bare face held directly up to the camera, with nothing to hide or distract from it.

The kitchen grew completely dark around us. Her breath evened out against my chest. Headlights moved across the ceiling. I thought for a moment she had fallen asleep standing up, like a horse. My chin still rested on her hair. She had promised she had not seen him, and would not speak to him again. That it was over. Large shadows trembled on the wall. A distant foghorn. I tried to place the exact feeling of having her in my arms. Was it happiness? Comfort? Did it hurt? Would it someday begin to hurt? I felt trapped by the unsureness that had followed me for as long as I could remember. I did not even know if I should still be mad. The distressed, red color of his penis haunted me not because of its indecency, but because of its garishness.

SUNLIGHT STREAMED through the window. I blinked, remembering where I was: Michigan, the Midwest. The shit smell had gone from the air, or else permeated it so thoroughly that I would blanch at the freshness outside. Birds chirped. The lake plashed rhythmically against the retaining wall in the yard. It reminded me, in my awakening haze, of the *crisp crisp crisp* of Kimia's feet in winter snow. Our super was always the last man in Brooklyn to shovel the sidewalk. Her place beside me in the bed was empty. I raised up on my elbows. She stood in front of the large window in a mismatched bikini with a steaming mug held in front of her, looking out at the lake. Her red bikini bottom was loose on her hips. The blue-striped top was tied with a bow in back. I had no idea why she would wear them together, instead of with their matching pair. Perhaps it was a very early sign of dementia.

"You're up," I said.

She smiled. "There's coffee on the stove."

The sun brought out the lighter strands in her hair. I wanted her to come back to bed. I wanted the demented bikini gone, though it was growing on me as I watched her breathe in it. The slight bagginess slipping down as she brushed a string from her thigh.

"I'm going to sit in the sun," she said, and, still smiling, she moved across the room and out the side door. I watched through the window as she crossed the yard below the knotty shade of the white pine. It was diminished both in size and portentousness by the daylight. Kimia set her butt on the retaining wall, swung her legs over, and sat with them dangling above the water. She sipped her coffee, her body neat and contained in the swimsuit, her short hair piled behind her bandanna. I collapsed onto my back and stared at the ceiling. A large brown spider inched across, threatening to plummet onto my face. Did it even know it was upside down? I rolled out of bed, shoved aside the blanket, and walked in my underwear across the threadbare carpet to the bathroom.

The toilet was scrubbed clean. The cramped, stinking menace (which had led me to piss in the yard the night before) was gone. Kimia must have been up at dawn. I wondered if she had spent a few minutes watching me sleep. I looked in the mirror. Hello: nose, eyes, lips, hair. I turned to the toilet. My penis was a perfectly reasonable color, maybe half a shade darker than my thighs but nothing obscene. Had her ex ever had his professionally examined? Was there a strange, disturbing part of my anatomy that Kimia silently put up with? No. I hoped not. I shook off, flushed the toilet, and went to the kitchen and poured myself a cup of coffee.

Kimia raised her eyebrows when I came outside.

"They're boxers," I said, crossing the lawn to join her. "It's like a swimsuit. Besides"—I gestured to the empty road—"there are only three or four other people in Michigan, and they're all asleep." I sat close to her on the wall so our hips touched. A few dark, downy hairs glimmered on her kneecaps. The front flap of my boxers gaped open, pubic hair peeking forth. She tucked her chin into her neck and blushed. She was wearing turquoise earrings along with her turquoise rings and the mismatched bikini. She looked like she was about to abscond to an art colony in New Mexico. I kissed the side of her head. Whitecaps showed on Lake Michigan in the distance. The water below our feet plashed on. "Is this a natural formation?" I asked, patting the concrete below her butt, and her butt.

Kimia nodded. "If you break it open there are crystals inside."

THE SCREEN DOOR banged shut behind us and I pressed her against the stove. She wrapped her calf around my knee and squeezed, sending pain shooting up my thigh. Our teeth collided. Her head fell back. I kissed along the tendons in her neck, feeling her short, sharp breaths. I ran my tongue down to the salty point between her breasts. The skin on her chest was flushed. She squirmed against me. A truck roared past and the windows rattled. I untied the back of her top. She pulled it over her head and tossed it away, hard, so it hit the fridge, slid down, and crumpled on the linoleum. She stared at me boldly, but with a pinprick of fear, like always.

The truck's roar seemed to continue and vibrate in the air. I caught her nipple between my teeth. Her skin was hot, with the sharp smell of herself below her perfume. She began to tremble—her muscles tensing as she tried to stop. She had been abused by a Sunday school teacher in her church from the ages of four to seven. Week after week, brought by her unknowing parents, before she could even begin to understand. They had converted and this was what they received in return. She ran her nails down the back of my skull, catching something tender. I winced, looking up. Her eyes were fixed on the wall behind my head. I wanted to bring a great and eradicating safety down upon her. A darkness. An erasure. I picked her up, carried her to the bed, and tossed her down on the faded blanket. She pushed the red bikini bottom off. She was always in a hurry at first, as if something might go wrong, I might transform. And some things were off limits: licking her vagina, looking closely at her vagina. She had told me this before we had sex for the first time, assuring me that she still did find pleasure in it, and want it, there were just moments. Punctuation marks, the occasional full stop.

Sometimes I found her so beautiful I wanted to kill the whole world.

Naked, she curled around my waist and dragged down my boxers. She caught my penis in her mouth, glanced up at me, and forced it as far down her throat as it would go. My spine stretched backward. Again I saw the ceiling, the spider distant now in its corner web, watching us with its dim, myriad eyes. The room began to list beneath me, like a boat at sea. I took hold of Kimia's shoulders and pushed her back. I lay my body flat on top of hers, trying to touch every inch of her, pinning her shoulders with my shoulders, gripping the sides of her head, her lips slick against my ear.

The unblemished parts of her childhood surrounded us: old unmatched furniture, doilies, a cordless telephone. She jerked in her breath when I pushed inside her. "Stay here," I whispered.

A BREEZE CAME off the lake late in the afternoon. It rustled the curtains and summoned us from our books. Earlier, I had tried to swim, and Kimia had laughed as I waded farther and farther out, the length of a football field, with the water still below my waist.

"We'll go to the dunes tomorrow," she said.

But now we were hungry and in no mood to cook. She put on jean shorts and a dark orange T-shirt over her bikini. The sun made the early summer grass look so green it was electric, like a single spark could ignite the Chevy Volt and the whole surface of the earth. We walked past the park into town. Deer grazed between the houses. They watched us with the pointed suspicion of locals, slapping flies away with their floppy ears. The hardware store appeared to have been closed for a long time, though rows of hammers and screws and light fixtures were still visible behind the window.

"This isn't even a town," Kimia said. "How did I used to think it was a town?"

Shay's Chophouse, Onekama's lone restaurant, was a three-story Victorian house with someone, Shay him- or herself, probably, still living on the upper floors. A cursive *Open* sign glowed pink in the window. Two cops shared a basket of calamari on the deck. They looked up, and their eyes lingered on Kimia's face, flicked back to mine, and then returned, satisfied, to the red basket and small cups of tartar sauce. I held the door for Kimia. She slipped past me and I wondered if she had lost weight. We had hardly slept in the weeks after I found the text messages, between our fights and reconciliations and fights again. She stopped in the doorway and we stood looking up at the jumble of strange objects on the walls. Huge leaping fish mounted on wood, vine plants spilling from the windowsills, antique glass bottles arranged from shortest to tallest, porcelain birds fluttering up from the shoulders of a figurine Saint Francis. It was as if several grandmothers had decorated all at once, each refusing to bend to the vision of the others.

"Go ahead and sit anywhere you like," the waiter said, appearing from the dark restroom hallway. At first I thought he was a random stranger who had come in to use the bathroom. His inch-long brown hair was fitted like a sock atop his doughy head. He wore jeans and a plain blue T-shirt. His belly stretched the fabric. No apron, black sneakers. A tender pouch of skin below his chin.

"Maybe a booth?" he asked, since we still had not moved.

Kimia nudged me with her elbow. "A booth is perfect," she said.

He led us in a determined trundle to a booth in the corner. Then, with the same doggedness, he filled our water glasses, straightened our silverware, nodded to himself, and returned to the kitchen.

"You can't just stare at people," she said, after he had gone. "He probably thinks you're going to murder him."

"*Murder*," I said. "Would I follow him home?"

She sighed, and turned to her menu. *An Uncompromised Dining Experience* was written in script across the top. Along the bottom, below the pizza toppings, *Uncompromised* was defined as *Possessing great character, quality, or origin; not counterfeit; authentic; real.*

"The irony is almost Zenlike," I said.

Kimia did not answer.

After a few minutes, the waiter reappeared. He dug a pad from the front pocket of his jeans. He flipped it open and beamed at us as if he had never seen us before. He had to be a relative of Shay's. A nephew or cousin who could not make it out in the real world. "Our special tonight is all-you-can-eat pasta. Carbonara or Alfredo, with salad and breadsticks."

I pictured a huge vat in the kitchen being stirred by a boy with a stick. "Does it come out in rounds?" I asked. "Or will there be a very large bowl?"

Confusion clouded his eyes. His pen hovered.

"The pasta," I said. Across the table, I could see Kimia doing everything in her power to keep from apologizing.

"Well, once you finish one plate, I'll just ask if you'd like another," he said.

"Perfect." I nodded. "I'll have the cheeseburger."

Mercifully, Kimia ordered the Alfredo and gave him her purest, most gentle smile as he collected our menus.

"Do you have to torture him?" she asked, watching his rounded back disappear into the kitchen.

"We finally found it," I said. "The last dumb, innocent heart of America. He didn't even ask if we wanted drinks."

She looked away, and I realized I had gone too far. Cruelty in any form cut her like a knife. Reading about the worsening violence in the West would leave her silent for hours, pressing the pads of her fingertips together. I thought of her great-grandfather, Ben Raafat, the first and only Muslim in this small town. Perhaps her empathy flowed from him.

"I got an offer to shoot a wedding in August," she said. "In Hawaii."

I sighed.

"It's a lot of money." She picked at the corner of her napkin. "Just for three days, you know, they want everything to be . . . perfect."

"That's good," I said. "August. We don't have anything in August." I tried to smile—it *was* good, we had rent and bills, and a week apart was not so horrible—but a pall had fallen over the table. Two years before, at the very beginning of our relationship, she shot a wedding in Key West, and while she was gone I slept with a poet at a party in Astoria. For months after, I would not let her leave, and now when she went I thought of her in a hotel room thinking of me with someone else, and the guilt drew me up in knots so tight parts of my body manifested the feeling: fingers interlocked, squeezed at the knuckles, legs wound together, toes digging into the soles of my shoes. I did not want her to have to trust me. I did not want to have to trust her.

Some mistakes do not go away, no matter how hard you try.

II

Make inside your heart a room

We came back to the cabin after our daughter was born. We rented a larger, safer car and split the trip over two days, staying the night with Kimia's sister and her husband in Syracuse before taking the northern route across Canada. At dinner, I watched the sisters laugh and reminisce, and fought back images in my mind of their tangled, sweaty, nearly identical limbs. Her husband kept asking me about Montana, what time of year to go, how far it was from the Redoubt, if it was safe, if the fishing was really all they said it was. We left early the next morning, but still it was nearly dark by the time we arrived in Onekama, and Gigi was fast asleep in her car seat.

Kimia's aunt and uncle, both high school teachers, had been at the cabin the week before, and left the key for us under the doormat. I knew the toilet water inside would be as clear and clean as a mountain stream. It had only been three years since our first visit, but the cabin, along with us, seemed to have grown up. It looked more upstanding in the dusk, as if it had been given a touch of paint and told that it was beautiful.

Kimia raised her eyebrows at me. As silently as possible, we eased out of the car. I opened the back door like a surgeon and extracted Gigi from her car seat. A bit of spittle bubbled on her sleeping lips. Her chin rested on her chest. A shock of black hair on the top of her head. She looked, I thought, exactly like her mother, right down to the way she tucked her head to blush. Others disagreed, and really it was just a tiny scrunched baby face, but I was trying to find a context for all the love I felt. I lifted her out and held her against my shoulder. Her warmth passed through my skin down to my toes.

Kimia unfolded our travel crib by the bed in the living room. She made a nest of blankets and I lay Gigi down. Just like that, we were home. Everything looked much the same: the mismatched old furniture, the doilies, the large window and the violet-tinged horizon. "I've never been so happy to smell dust," Kimia whispered.

We tiptoed back and forth to the car, bringing in our luggage, putting the groceries into the fridge and cupboards, and neatening the blankets on the bed. Then Kimia pulled me into the inner bedroom. We made love on the floor with the door wide open. Kimia completely naked, me in my undershirt and socks in case I had to hop up to check on the baby, both of us struggling not to make the slightest noise. Much of Kimia's fear and shame about her body had disappeared since giving birth. Sometimes I found her bottomless in front of the mirror, her hands cupped over her groin, a look of rapt concentration on her face, as if she were exploring some new and profound internal terrain. A silent world. Her vagina felt different to me, too. It was not an aircraft hangar, as my brother had disgustingly warned, but it was roomier. Gentler also, and with a sort of inward gravity. I felt as if I were being drawn inside her. As if motherhood had made her strong enough to hold us both.

"Stay here," she whispered, smiling down at me.

GIGI WOKE US at midnight and remained awake until dawn, when she slept for twenty minutes and then woke again, screaming so ferociously that we decided we might as well start the day. I held her and made coffee while Kimia showered, and then we traded places. The shower itself was a nightmare. A trickle, really, that left me, after my sleepless night, feeling greasy and vulnerable. We spent the rest of the morning trying to entertain Gigi with toys and music and the shallow lake and the white pine, all to no avail. Finally, we decided to take her to the dunes, hoping the drive would put her to sleep.

But she had had enough of that the day before. She was all energy. She pointed and cooed out the window at a flash of beach, the boats dotting the water, a distant tanker moving implacably southward. The land grew more wild as we sped north along the lake. Fewer and fewer houses, bigger and bigger trees. The startling burst of a patch of wildflowers. Thirty miles passed in a blur of Gigi's exclamations, with Kimia swiveling around in the passenger seat to explain each new thing: a tractor, an abandoned schoolhouse, a black cow. Even I was feeling awake by the time we arrived.

The turn came just before Glen Arbor. Two teenage girls were taking a selfie in front of the national park sign. Smiling broadly, they looked more sincere than I had ever been at their age. I found us a spot in the wide tree-ringed lot, beside another family readying themselves for a childproofed expedition: juice boxes, sunscreen, granola bars. The two young sons were pelting each other with pinecones. The older boy hit the younger in the face and then ran screaming to his mother before the younger could react. It was impossible for me to imagine that Gigi would one day be capable of violence and deceit; I was so used to her explosively expressing whatever emotion she currently held. We got out, and Kimia put on the organic baby carrier that my parents had sent. I loaded Gigi inside, winked at her, and stuck out my tongue. I snugged her wide-brimmed sun cap on her head. I slipped her sunglasses over her tiny ears. She grinned at me like a drunken pop star.

A concrete path led through the trees. I followed Kimia, carrying our day bag of camera, diapers, sunscreen, sippy cup, water, wipes, blanket, extra bags for the dirty diapers, sanitizer, baby lotion (which Kimia used more than Gigi), baby food, and two sad, hastily prepared cheese sandwiches. The forest ended abruptly at the foot of the first dune, whose flank climbed precipitously for more than three hundred feet. It had been dubbed Empire by a zealous park ranger in the fifties, perhaps a midwestern man like our former waiter, whose face, out of guilt, lingered vividly in my mind. We trudged up the side in a thousand other footprints. The sun was hot on my back and my shirt stuck to my skin. The sand sank beneath my feet with each plunging step upward. Shouts and exclamations of similarly humbled travelers came from ahead. Thankfully, Gigi was fascinated. She twisted her head around beneath her cap and grinned as she slumped forward and back with each of her mother's labored steps.

"Enjoy it," I told her. "You're going to have to walk for *years*."

The ridge, which we reached after about a decade, was crowded with tourists holding up cell phones to capture the rolling expanse of dunes: a miniature wavelike desert, surrounded by forest on three sides and bright blue Lake Michigan on the fourth. To the east, a white barn sat in the center of a clearing in the forest. The juxtaposition between the barn and the dunes made it seem like one of them was fake. "Do you see the lake?" Kimia asked. "Do you see the lake?"

Gigi crowed. I dug the water bottle from the bag and took a long drink, splashing a bit on my chin and leaning into the cool breeze.

"Should we try to make it to the beach?" Kimia said.

"We can try," I said skeptically. It was almost two miles on the sand, in the sun, with the baby and our bags. Most of the tourists did not go any farther than the top of Empire. But we were young parents, hearty, with a lot of world to show our little girl. We traded burdens, me kneeling to hoist Gigi onto my back, and Kimia slinging the bag over her shoulder. Going down was nothing—a series of hops—but then almost immediately we were climbing back up another, only slightly smaller dune. My thighs began to ache. But each time I slowed I was buoyed forward by a small knee in my back. Gigi crowed triumphantly. She took on the character of a kindly but ruthless captain, propelling the wheezing ship of my body across the waves of sand. Kimia was similarly buoyant. Dropping down the second dune, she took off her shoes and the bag and did a cartwheel, landing in a laughing heap. One of her turquoise rings flew far ahead of her. She pushed herself up, still laughing, and retrieved it. The ecstasy she found in motherhood sometimes worried me, as if in her happiness she might leave me behind, but that day it carried me along. I wanted nothing more than to be packhorse for those two females, helping them to the shore.

At the top of the third dune, we surprised a group of University of Michigan frat boys, shirtless and grappling as they tried to compose a human pyramid. Kimia agreed to take their picture and we waited until they managed, briefly, to right themselves, before collapsing into what looked like the precursor to a sordid sexual act. "Thanks!" and "Cute baby!" they called after us. To which I nodded, as I always did, knowing they actually meant *timeless, incomparable.*

The slope evened out onto a wide plain spotted with salt grass. We found ourselves alone. The nearest figures were small and distant to the east. By the time we reached the final peak, I had to shade my eyes and squint to see anyone at all. The lake spread out before us to the curve of the horizon. It was so vast it reminded me of the Atlantic, save for its richer bluer hue. I lowered my hands to my knees, sucking in oxygen, and let Gigi look over my shoulder at the white-crested waves. Kimia turned in a full circle, then she leaned over to kiss my sweaty cheek. Her eyes sparkled devilishly. She straightened and ran plunging down toward the water, shedding her clothes as she went. By the time she reached the beach, only her black panties remained. She shucked these off just as easily, and I watched her dance into the waves, her butt so pale against the rest of her skin that it looked like a separate piece of clothing.

"Look," I said to Gigi. "Look at your mama."

We ate our sandwiches in the sand, and then Kimia, still naked, lay on her back and watched the few tattered clouds moving west across the sky. Gigi sprinkled her legs with fistfuls of sand. The warmth of the sun reached down and held us in its palm.

"It was like this," Kimia said. "It felt just like this."

The waves crashed and receded in their relentless, beautiful pattern. I understood what she meant, though I had no time from my own childhood to compare. Not that it had been unhappy, I was just never content. I had always wanted more: more freedom, more time, more control. More from my parents, my brother, my friends, and most of all myself. It was only in the past year, at the age of thirty-two, that I felt I could stand still.

The foam surf swirled hypnotically and my mind drifted

from past to present and back again. Time felt like it was speeding up, and skipping things in between. I was not sure I was the same person I had been even the week before. I was shedding layers, fatherhood revealing each new nakedness. Gigi burbled in the sand. She was slathered in sunscreen, fed, watered. She made no move to eat anything or drown. We were safe. I began to doze off, and was nearly asleep when I felt a presence behind us. I turned. A man was standing atop the dune, looking down.

"*Kim*," I hissed.

She opened her eyes. "Shit." She scrambled for her clothes, trying to cover herself, and I scooped up Gigi, who instantly burst into tears. The man remained motionless, unbothered by having been discovered, as if he had every right to watch. His features were hidden by the angle of the sun. I remembered the man in the truck on our first day in Onekama, his eyes shadowed by the low bill of his baseball cap. And others whose eyes had held Kimia too long. I stared up, trying to force him to look at me instead. He folded his arms across his chest. His shadow stretched behind him. There was something looming and terrible in his figure, like a judge casting a cruel, irreversible verdict. The fear I sometimes felt walking with Kimia down an unfamiliar street at night flooded in. What did he see? What would he do? He stared unwaveringly, staying until she was fully dressed. Then, slowly, casually, he walked south along the ridge.

My heart pounded. I wanted to fly up the wall of sand and pummel him. I wanted to crush his throat between my knees.

I wanted to go back in time and make him not exist. But I was rooted to the sand.

The safety I dreamt of bringing Kimia, and our daughter, was only that: a dream.

"We should go," Kimia said, her face strained, her bra twisted in the sand beside her.

BY THE TIME we got back to the car, it was dark, and our exhaustion, combined with the menacing encounter, had passed us through the stage of irritation to outright hostility. We argued about why we had not brought more food. We argued about why we had left so late in the day. I asked whose idea it had been, anyway, to go all the way to the beach and take off all their clothes. Gigi wailed as I buckled her into the car seat. Kimia stood back, shaking the sand from her hair and swiping it off her thighs.

"You need to make sure she's sitting up straight," she said. "Not slumped forward."

"She's tired. Look." I demonstrated how secure all the clips and straps were. Kimia shouldered past me and knelt. She whispered reassuringly to Gigi as she redid everything.

"She was fine," I said, getting into the driver's seat.

As soon as we were moving, Gigi fell asleep. The black trees on either side of the road reached toward the sliver of moon. I drove in silence. The universe yawned overhead, as if fate were an open mouth waiting to bite down. The whole country was shaken, what right did I have to feel differently?

We lived in its heaving, tectonic cruelty, and the love flowing up between. I turned onto the county highway. A small gleaming market and gas station slid past. Two old men sat on a bench beside an old-time soda machine, staring into the darkness. It was the kind of thing you hoped to see in the Midwest. I cracked the window to let the cool night air in.

Stars glittered. Satellites blinked in pale imitation. My anger began to fade. I knew I was not actually mad at Kimia, I was mad at myself, and had reached a limit in my own body.

But the cabin, food, and bed were waiting for us. We would never see the man again. Nor the other from her past. Everything would not be taken from me. I hardly ever thought of danger. The people dying on the news were distant, strangers. Glowing mile markers flashed by. I breathed the fresh air. I imagined what it might be like to live in a place like this. Or farther north: Alaska, the Yukon. In deepest woods, with no one around but the wolves. My parents had moved to Montana the year I was born.

After a time, Kimia spoke. "I should start taking weddings again soon when we get back." Her eyes gleamed in the dashboard glow. Her features were lost in shadow. "They'll stop asking if I don't."

A little hardness formed in the back of my throat. I did not answer.

She turned to the window and her head drifted back to the headrest. "We can talk about it later." Her words drowsed off. The road wound over a small hill past Tweddle Farm. A sign advertised CHERRY BERRY PIE, CHERRY BERRY JAM. The tires hummed on the pavement beneath us. I wondered if my parents had ever had a day like this when I was Gigi's age. If everyone did. Hiking too long, loving too much. If their wounds had ever healed, or if you just live with the scars, sometimes hidden, sometimes not. Fragile in this world with so much to lose.

WE'RE IN THIS TOGETHER
YOU KNOW, GOD

EVERYONE I TELL ABOUT HER THINKS I MUST'VE DRANK while I was pregnant. That I poisoned her in the womb like her older brother who is dumb and often overwhelmed but so gentle with animals it would break your heart. Even Dr. Hulce at the Cleary Center who it's his job to know when people are lying asks me over and over if I ingested anything or had any kind of relapse.

"She's just bad," I tell him.

He tips his head toward the window. Two crows sit in the old maple tree over the lawn. Dr. Hulce is going bald and the top of his scalp has a grayness to it that worries me. "How so?"

"There's just badness in the world," I tell him. "I learned

that from her. It's always been here. Maybe you'd call it the devil, or a demon. Some people it catches them before they're even born."

"Remember this is your daughter, Mrs. Davis," he says. "We're talking about your daughter."

I stare at the light shining on his gray scalp.

What I remember are the horses.

"We want to get her well. That's why we have these meetings. Because we're trying to get your daughter well." He looks at me and his eyes have a grayness to them, too, like he's dealt with so many gray things that it's gotten inside him. He opens the folder on his desk and smooths the top paper. "She won the talent show here last week. Did you know that? She sang a song about Jesus conquering the grave."

My hands go cold in my lap. I know the song. *Grave where's your victory, and death where's thy sting?* I used to sing it over her crib. She has no right to profit by it. And why would they even have a talent show in a place like this? Every time I come I wonder why there aren't more bars on the windows. Why the children aren't more carefully locked away.

"And then what?" I ask.

Dr. Hulce lifts the top paper—a chart covered in scrawled writing—and looks at the next. He sighs. Outside, the crows are silent and still. "Then she climbed up on the wall cabinets and hissed at everyone."

I nod. That's her. That's my little girl. I used to think she was my punishment but she's far outpaced the crimes.

IT STARTED for Buddy and me when we got the horse farm twelve years ago. Inherited from Buddy's uncle who thought to give us a second, or third, or fourth chance. And for the first two of those years we took it. Losing our anger and weakness to the work, letting it wring us out and even cleanse us, with sweet dumb Jim following at our heels and helping in small ways where he could.

I can't say we got rich or fore-doubled our shares, but neither did we run the farm into the ground as so many had said we would. When Cindy was born we had a broodmare band of twelve, along with the stallion Boonlight Dancer, an NCHA Futurity finalist who we offered out for breeding consideration. All of us living together on thirty healthy acres in the shadow of Mount Rainier. My God. Those years. There are moments I remember like paintings hung up in a museum: Buddy coming in from working a colt awash in sunlight, dirt on his forehead and straw in the cuffs of his shirt, looking astonished and like so much of a man that I thought it was possible I'd become a real working woman, too.

It's feelings like that that hang you, and it wasn't long before I was in what my mother called *a bad way*. The pregnancy laid me up for three months and the whole weight of the farm fell on Buddy. His eyes got frantic then, stirring up bad memories as he tried to keep the end from slipping out from underneath him. But he managed somehow. And it all seemed worthwhile when we looked down at baby Cindy for the first time. She was a perfect-looking child, even right there after she was born. Blond hair curling thickly in the afterbirth, a button nose, and bright sparkling eyes. All the nurses came in to coo over her, and Buddy couldn't stop his blushing. For a moment he must've fancied himself like Boonlight Dancer, and thought that after such a fine performance it wouldn't be unreasonable to be put out to stud.

But this story is not about Buddy's failings, nor mine, though there have been plenty to go around.

I saw nothing unusual in Cindy as a baby. She had a tendency to pinch hard at the teat like I thought only a boy would do, but I didn't linger on it and she grew into a sharp, quick-eyed child. Able to read by three and always watching out at the world, digging her little teeth into her lower lip. She learned so fast that Buddy and I supposed she might go to college someday.

The first hints of meanness came soon after. She squalled terribly when left alone, and took it as a personal insult when either of us showed love to any other living thing. Poor Jim took her earliest abuse. He was twelve then, and too big for her to hurt, but she discovered she could hurt herself and blame him, and we'd do the hurting for her.

I remember the first time clearly. Coming into the living room one winter morning to find her lying on her back on the carpet, a cut across her forehead, a trickle of blood down her cheek, with Jim sitting on the couch looking helpless and confused in front of the frost-covered windows, more or less as he always did. She lifted a tiny trembling finger, and anger lit up my chest. "He pushed me," she said. "After I wouldn't watch what he wanted."

The anger kept me from thinking clearly. The sound wasn't even on, on the TV. I called Buddy in and when he saw the damage to his little girl he didn't hesitate to take off his belt, though we'd never had to punish Jim that way before. I brought Cindy into the kitchen, washed the cut, and dabbed on peroxide. Then I held her in my lap as Jim screamed and cried in the other room. The peroxide must've stung something awful but Cindy didn't seem to notice. She sat listening with a look of perfect contentment, blinking placidly at each crack of the belt.

"THE HISSING ISN'T UNUSUAL," Dr. Hulce says. "A lot of the girls imitate cats. Never dogs. You'll never hear one bark. But hissing, curling up the spine, clawing out at anyone who comes close. They relate to cats because they share the same reactive attachment disorder. They're affectionate and want all your attention until something puts them off, and then . . ." He raises his eyebrows. "Well, you know. Anything can happen."

Reactive attachment disorder. The doctors here are so good at putting big words on things. I've got a whole list of the diagnoses at home: oppositional defiant disorder, comorbid conduct disorder, ADHD. I think they're supposed to make me feel better, but all I want is for one of them to look her in the face and recognize the evil looking back.

"She's no cat," I tell him quietly.

AT FIVE, we had her start helping with the horses. Thinking a third hand would be a boon to us since there was so little Jim could do. We even fantasized about her taking over the farm someday. Using her sharpness to make it grow, buying out our neighbors, increasing our breeding capabilities. On humid nights, Buddy spoke of racehorses. His name in derby lights.

I showed Cindy how to water and feed the mares, and how to treat them so they wouldn't fear her hand. Moving always in a steady way, speaking as to friends, letting them keep track of her both in eye and nose. She took to it quickly and soon we turned over the evening watering to her, thinking it a simple place for her to start.

Is there no greater fool than a mother?

High Brow Cat was the queen of our little broodmare band, and always my favorite. A high-backed sorrel with a proud temperament. Often she showed her disgust in visitors by flicking her tail, turning around, and presenting them with her lofty rump. But always she let me ride her, and nickered prettily when I came near. Within a month of Cindy's watering, I noticed a change in her demeanor. Instead of strutting out to the center of the field when set free to graze as she usually did, she'd find a near place at the fence and stand there dully, sometimes even leaning her forehead against the cross-posts. When I stroked her muzzle, she hardly seemed to notice.

Fearing infection, I summoned the vet. He found nothing wrong save exhaustion and dehydration, and questioned our feeding and watering patterns. A weaselly, superior little man, his suggestion touched a raw nerve—many in Buddy's family believed we'd kill off the horses with our negligence—and I nearly ran him off the property. Still, I took his advice and increased the mares' rations, adding another full third on top of what I poured for them in the morning.

High Brow Cat seemed to recover, and all went well for a month or so, until a nagging suspicion, one I wouldn't even allow to fully form in my mind, led me to follow Cindy out to the barn one night. Feeling like no kind of a mother, I hid in the shadow of the door and watched her walk past High Brow Cat's stall to the washing area. She unwound the hose from the reel, checked the nozzle, and turned on the water. Then she approached the stall slowly. We couldn't afford fancy automatic waterers, so a five-gallon bucket hung just inside the stall's gate, with a heating coil underneath to keep it from freezing in the winter.

Cindy made strange high-pitched sounds in her throat as she lifted the gate latch. I supposed they were meant to be soothing, but they made me want to back out into the coolness of the yard and flee to the nearest church, or liquor store. She went inside and stood in front of the bucket, speaking softly to High Brow Cat. The horse came up to her side. Moving slowly and steadily as I'd taught, Cindy lifted the hose and squeezed the nozzle, setting forth a stream of water. Except the stream didn't go into the bucket; it splashed on the ground beside it. At first I thought it was an accident, that she'd misjudged and would correct herself, but then High Brow Cat lowered her snout and licked at the stream, and Cindy drew the nozzle back out of reach.

Water puddled in the straw and ran toward the drain.

The other horses shifted uneasily in their stalls, as if they'd come to expect this nightly ritual. I watched, transfixed, as the puddle grew. Cindy let the water run and run, approximating the filling of the bucket, as if she thought we had some way of checking how much had been poured out. Growing desperate, High Brow Cat nuzzled her shoulder. Cindy responded with a hiss so sudden and sharp it made me jump, and the horse jerked its head away.

I backed out of the barn and walked quickly, nearly running, down the drive to the house. I know I should have confronted her then, but I was frightened of the cruelty I'd witnessed, and confused, and ashamed. I told Buddy what I'd seen and in the telling it grew even stranger and more unreal. He viewed it as a product of small childhood, of not yet understanding the results of her actions, and confronted Cindy gently, thinking the solution was simply that she should no longer water the horses on her own, at least not until she was old enough for the responsibility.

I lay awake all that night, wondering what I'd done wrong as a mother.

A LARGE MALE NURSE with a shaved head, beard, and tattoos around his thick wrists leads me from Dr. Hulce's office to the security check outside the Family Room. JEREMIAH LAMB, his badge reads, as if his mother were a Bible. Most of the nurses at the Cleary Center are large and male, and look like they ride motorcycles on their off days. They have to be. Children are stronger than you think.

"Do you know her?" I ask, handing him my purse and keys. "Cindy?"

He motions for me to come through the metal detector. Then he shrugs. "She's never bit me. I mostly keep track of the biters."

I smile, appreciating the honesty. Many of the nurses here blame you for your child, as if it must've been something you did. As if just because you carried them in your womb you shouldn't be afraid of them. A plate-glass window looks in on the blue and gray walls of Zebra Ward. Calming colors, I assume, though they make me want to scream. A lone large teenage boy is sitting on the beanbag chair in the corner. A book is open on his lap but he's focused on punching his thigh in a steady, hard, rhythmic manner. Two orderlies appear on the near side of the ward, carrying a small squirming mass by the arms and legs toward the hall at the other end.

The large boy's fist freezes in midair and he looks up, excitement animating his oblong face. "Chew the wall!" he says, as they pass. He lowers his voice as the smaller struggling boy catches his eye. "You *better* chew the wall."

Jeremiah places my belongings into a metal tray and shakes his head. "One of them figured out there's a corner in isolation where the wall is rounded enough to get your mouth on. Now as soon as they get in they go to that corner and chew. It's like a competition. There's nothing else to do in there." He stops, remembering who he's talking to. "I think we have a contractor coming to look at it next week."

I wave my hand. "As long as they can't chew their way out."

He looks at me levelly for a moment, then opens the Family Room door and motions for me to go in. "I'll be right here if you need," he says.

I pause in front of the nubbly rubber threshold. The first step is always the hardest. I tell myself, Okay, you can do this. And then it's two weeks before you have to think about it again. Which of course is a lie. I can count the seconds on one hand that go by between when I think about Cindy.

I step forward. The door clicks shut behind me. I'm alone.

The Family Room is a drab sterile box with a rubber table and rubber chairs. The walls are bare and gray. There's no wood nor nails, nothing sharp, no rounded corners, nothing to chew on or stab with. It's a neutral de-weaponized zone between the public portion of the Cleary Center, where the doctors have their offices, and the locked wards where the children are kept. And it's the only place I can see my daughter. Twice a month for sixty minutes.

A crate of games sits in the corner. This means Cindy has been on good behavior. When she's been bad, the games disappear. I pull one of the chairs back from the table and sit and look at the opposite door, knotting my fingers in my lap and thinking, *Chew the wall.*

WE DIDN'T EVEN QUESTION the first time she got trampled. It was a year after the watering incident. Jim had learned to stay out of her way, more or less, and everything was going well, though the farm work plus all the extra attention Cindy demanded had begun to wear us thin. Then one morning we found her on her back in the corral with a broken arm and a bright purple bruise across her shoulder. Buddy carried her to his truck and we drove, ignoring the speed limit, to the ZoomCare in Centralia, where they fitted her with a cast and the young doctor remarked how amazing it was that she didn't cry. Not a single tear.

An accident, we figured, sitting in the kitchen later that afternoon. Who knows what she'd been doing in there, but horses spook easily sometimes, and thank God she wasn't hurt worse. The mare, a dapple named Bueno Starlight, had broken an ankle. Shattered it, with bone sticking out through the hide. There was nothing for it, and Buddy put her down that very night.

The second trampling came only a month after Cindy's cast was removed. In the barn this time, where she wasn't even supposed to be since the watering incident. Miraculously, she suffered nothing worse than a gash across her stomach, but the mare, a yearling named Smart Little Lena, had somehow come down on a nail. It was driven all the way up through her heel to the quick of the bone.

I still think about this. How Cindy must have placed the nail, and aimed it, amid the flurry of hooves as the frightened horse bucked and stamped. What viciousness must have steadied her mind, what poison. I picture the look of concentration on her face, even with the prospect of her own death so near at hand.

We called in the vet and he spent two hours with Smart Little Lena before finally giving up. The nail was too deep. If he took it out, she'd never walk again. If he left it in, the infection would kill her slow and painful. We gave him permission to end her suffering.

And just like that, in a single season, we'd lost one-sixth of our assets. We forbade Cindy from going near the horses anymore, and ordered her to remain in the house unless accompanied by one of us. She was no longer even allowed into the small fenced-in front yard without permission.

I lay awake many nights that spring. The scope of what she was capable of was slowly dawning on me. I began to avoid her. I couldn't reconcile her face with the lost mares and the sounds of Jim's cries, which I'd come to know in my heart were unwarranted. Perhaps that was the worst of it: how she'd made us her accomplice. I expect Buddy will be haunted by those whippings until the day he dies, as will I.

THE DOOR OPPOSITE me opens and there, standing in a rectangle of fluorescent light, is Cindy. She's grown since my last visit. She stands very straight, her chin thrust forward, eyes bright and curious. Her blond ponytail is fixed in place with a pink clip. I can't tell what she's thinking, like I can with Jim or

Buddy. She hides everything behind a mask of doll-like perfection, prettier than I ever was as a child.

My mother used to say that if you could remember how bad childbirth was, you'd never do it again. At the time, I'd thought it was just one of the silly things she said to fill the air, but now I wonder if the whole tragedy of parenthood isn't wrapped up within it. All the pain my children have caused, starting from the moment they tore my vagina to come into the world, fades into unreality at the sight of their faces.

Cindy looks down at her feet on the linoleum. I hardly notice the nurse escorting her, and I stand and nod blankly when he asks if I'm comfortable being left alone. She's as tall as my chest. The pink dress she's wearing was a Christmas present last year. It's gotten too short for her, and tight. A flood of worry closes my throat at what kind of boys she must be locked away with in here, like that fat one, punching his thigh.

She looks up into my eyes. "Hi, Mom," she says, and wraps her arms around my waist.

I touch the back of her head, blinking back tears, and wonder if we aren't all just animals, deep down.

SHE WAITED until late summer for her final, most terrible act. I don't know how long it was brewing inside her. Perhaps my ignoring her woke new stores of evil. Or perhaps there was never anything I could've done. Either way, she waited until the August nights were breezy and tinder-dry.

Buddy and I were shaken from sleep by the crackle of burning wood. An orange glow leapt across our upstairs window. Rolling out of bed and stumbling to the glass, I could feel the heat. The entire yard was lit as if by daylight. Black smoke swirled up from the barn, a monstrous tornado in reverse. Buddy and I looked at each other—our whole failed lives contained in that look—and then we ran down the stairs. Buddy went out the door; I called 911. Then I joined him on the lawn, dashing back and forth for buckets, the hose, before realizing it was too late.

The barn was engulfed in flame, and the crackling sound had been joined by the final shrieks of the horses. High Brow Cat, Boonlight Dancer, and all the rest. Dying as our dreams do, where they slept.

Cindy appeared in the night in her pink nightdress, dragging along her blue blanket. Her face was calm. She came to stand beside us. No match nor oil can in her hands, but we knew, and she knew we knew. That was the strangest part. She never feared punishment. It was like she thought the things she did would bring us closer together. She pressed her body against my thigh.

I grabbed her and flung her down, violently, into the dirt.

"Get away from me," I said.

BANANAGRAMS IS HER favorite game. She likes it because she doesn't have to wait her turn. She can just go, go, go. She pours the wooden squares from the yellow bag onto the table in front of us. Carefully, she makes sure each one is facedown. Then we draw out our twenty-one and she flips the plastic hourglass.

Being near her creates something like a traffic jam in my mind—all my thoughts piling up behind one another—and I've never been much for spelling, but I don't want her to win. I stare at the jumble of letters in front of me, trying to remember one single word. *VLOB. DOOCTIG.*

"Denise tells me something terrible is going to happen to me soon," Cindy says suddenly. "And there's nothing I can do to stop it."

I look up and find her bright eyes staring intently into mine. "Who's Denise?"

"A girl from Penguin Ward. She's twelve and fat and she's always taking off her clothes to show the boys."

It doesn't sound like a person anyone should listen to. "You've already made terrible things happen," I say quietly.

Cindy ignores me, as she always does when I bring up the past. "She says I'm going to bleed and bleed and it will never stop."

Bleed. *BLOOD.* The letters are staring up at me. I arrange them into a column. "You are going to bleed," I say. "But it will stop."

Her brow furrows. She looks down at the floor and bites her lip like she did when she was a baby, getting frustrated, angry. "I don't want to." She balls her fist, extends two knuckles, and begins to beat them on the edge of the table, shaking her letters.

Unconsciously, I lift my hand to comfort her. Sometimes when she gets like this she goes into what Dr. Hulce calls a catatonic state—all the life leaving her eyes, walking around expressionless in circles, refusing to stop, her legs continuing to move even if you pick her up. I know if I trigger one the staff will look down on me even more than they already do.

And still, I'm her mother. I can see red welts appearing on her fingers.

"Look." I point to her letters. "You have a *K*, that's your favorite. Can you think of a word with *K*?"

Cindy releases her lip. Her hand slows. The table stills. "None of the boys are going to fall in love with her anyway. Lucas said so. She's too fat."

"That's not nice."

She leans over the table, scrunches her forehead, and uses her fingertip to push the *K* in a snaking path through her letters. I can see her mind working. She begins to hum, the same hymn she used to win the talent show. *Grave where's your victory?* I remember how we thought she'd go to college someday, and again I feel the heat of tears behind my eyes.

"Too fat," she says softly. "Too fat, too fat."

Buddy refuses to come with me on these visits. He says he'd rather go to jail than come here. I picture him at home in our little apartment, sleeping in the sunlight on his bald rag of a pillow. He works nights now at Fred Meyer. The insurance wouldn't pay out after they discovered the barn fire was arson, and the sale of the farm didn't come to much once we'd squared our debts. It's been the worst on Jim. We hardly have the space for him, and he misses the horses dearly, still wakes nights to the sound of their screams.

"Kin!" Cindy says brightly, grouping the tiles. The word doesn't connect to her others like it's supposed to, nor is it a word she should ever be allowed to use, but I don't say anything. I think of old gray Dr. Hulce reminding me that she is my daughter. As if I could ever forget. As if . . . Her cheeks are flushed with excitement. She fingers the tiles, searching for another word. It's only been ten minutes and I'm ready to leave. But also a part of me would stay here forever, blocked off from the world. No past, no future. Sitting in a rubber chair across from my daughter. Playing games. Watching the sparks in her eyes.

PREY

I WAKE FROM A DREAM KNOWING THAT SOMEONE, OR SOME-thing, is in my bed. All the muscles in my arms and back are rigid. I roll over. A single lidless eye gleams on the pillow beside me, milk-chocolate-brown with an elliptical pupil, swollen now, in the near-dark. It's Voldemort, smiling at me with her long, double-hinged jaws.

I scramble out of bed, slivers of dawn leaking through the blinds and across my bare legs.

"Whatcha doing, girl?" I ask. "You have a bad dream?"

She's stretched as long as she can make herself, like a spear. It's a startling way to see her. Usually she's coiled or doing the S-slither. Her head on my pillow is next to an orange Cheetos stain, and her glossy gold and black body extends the length of the blue comforter and off the end of the bed. She's almost eight feet long. "You've grown," I tell her. It occurs to me that when we're lying side by side, she's a lot longer than I am.

I lift her midsection and drag her back to her tank under the window. She's at least a hundred pounds. Her skin is slick: not wet, but not quite dry. It's surprisingly cool, like spaghetti that's been left out overnight. She starts to curl around my arm. "You're too big for that, too," I say, pulling away.

Her tank runs the length of my wall. It has a heat lamp and fake foliage, a heated log, branches that she likes to drape herself over, and a pool to soak in. A Hermione Granger doll sits in the corner. I spend most of my extra money heating the tank and buying her food and toys. The lid is pushed open. I think back on last night: a meatball Hot Pocket, push-ups, some porn. Maybe I didn't latch the lid properly after I tried to feed her. The uneaten rat is gnawing a fake leaf by the pool.

"Bad snake," I whisper, kissing her face and putting her on her log. "Stay." I snap the lid shut.

I get back in bed and stare at the plastic stars on my ceiling.

"GO BACK TO SLEEP," my roommate Jasper growls when I pound on his door. He came with me when I bought Voldemort at Tropical Pet World four years ago. We were freshmen at the University of Montana—reading *Harry Potter* and smoking a lot of pot. We drew lightning bolts on the baby mice we fed her and said, "Expelliarmus," when we flushed her molted skin down the toilet. For a while, I said, "Expelliarmus," every time I flushed the toilet. I've always had trouble with girls.

"It's an emergency."

"You can come in here with us," his girlfriend Nancy calls. I consider it. The three of us tangled up, whispering and re-situating our bodies. They're both in good shape. She plays rugby. She has incredible breasts and they'd be swinging.

I listen to her and Jasper rolling out of bed and putting on clothes. I don't know what she sees in him. He's my best friend, but he's big and blocky and has a Neanderthal look, like he should be constantly grunting. He's the right kind of big, I guess. Not chunky, like me.

He mutters about replacing my antidepressants with Ambien as I lead them to my room. Nancy wears a pair of his boxers, yellow ducks floating on blue cotton. I've never seen a yellow duck in real life. Her short hair is spiked out every which way.

"She was right there." I point to the left side of my bed. "Stretched out straight as a spear."

"You let your snake in your bed?" Nancy asks.

"I didn't let her. I woke up and she was there. She scared me." I turn to Jasper. "I think there's something wrong with her. She hasn't eaten in weeks."

He scratches his mustache. It's new and he's proud of it. "She looks pretty healthy to me. I thought it was normal for pythons not to eat for weeks."

"Not in June," I reply. "They're supposed to eat a lot in the summer. And she's acting weird. You should have seen her all straight. It was unnatural."

"It's pretty weird that you have a giant snake in the first place," Nancy says. She doesn't know Voldemort like Jasper does. She and Jasper have only been together six months. I didn't think they'd make it this long. He's never been serious with anyone before.

"Take her to the vet if you're worried," Jasper says. "She could probably use a checkup."

I haven't taken her since she was a baby and they gave her pills for parasites. She wasn't even a foot long then. I toted her around in a little plastic case. Now she watches me from inside her heated log, her chocolate eyes blank.

WE DECIDE to carry her in a garbage bag to Cats on Broadway. It's only two blocks away. I don't have anything else that will fit her. I put some sand at the bottom so she'll feel at home. "What a big good girl," I coo, as we load her in. She writhes around, and it takes both of us to control the bag until she settles down.

"It's dark in there; she's probably sleeping," I say, to make myself feel better.

"This is ridiculous," Jasper says.

The bag is heavy and awkward and we end up dragging her through the grass. Around sprinkler heads and piles of dog shit. I'm glad our neighbors are at work.

The receptionist wears a salmon cardigan covered with

cat hair. Her red perm is coming loose in the summer heat. I picture little saucers of milk scattered around her apartment. Cats gross me out—licking themselves, coughing.

"I have an appointment for my python," I say.

She looks at the bag, starts to say something, stops, and slides a clipboard across the desk. "Fill these out. The doctor will be with you in a few minutes."

"Are vets really doctors?" Jasper asks, in a whisper, when we're seated in stained blue chairs against the wall. He was premed for three years until he flunked organic chemistry. The waiting room is empty. A single orange baseball cap hangs on a coat rack by the door. It looks like it's been there a long time. On the phone this morning, the receptionist told me they could squeeze me in because of a cancellation. Cat magazines are fanned across a plastic table.

"I think this place is just for cats," I whisper back.

I finish the forms and return them to the receptionist. She opens the file drawer by her feet and looks down helplessly at the jumble of manila folders inside. "There used to be another girl here, but she left town." This is a euphemism for going to the Redoubt. People still talk about moving to other cities, or going on vacation, but "left town" means joining up. Empty seats appear in my classes, and the professors shake their heads and cross the name off their roll sheet. It seems like everyone who's mad about anything finds a reason to go. More freedom, more justice, or some bullshit. As if large numbers of pissed-off men with guns ever led to justice.

Voldemort wakes and starts writhing again. Jasper pretends not to notice. I pull the bag closer to my chair. I was supposed to graduate last spring, but I failed some classes, so I have at least another year. I told my parents I'm double majoring. I can't imagine being qualified for anything more complex than filling a tortilla. If I joined up—not that I ever would—it'd be to make my life less pathetic.

The vet's a young guy with tortoiseshell glasses. His white sneakers squeak on the linoleum floor. "Creative, I like it," he says, when we haul the garbage bag in. He introduces himself as Dr. Gavin.

We gently spill Voldemort onto the steel table.

"She's a beauty," Dr. Gavin says. He runs his finger along her back, and she's embarrassed—under the bright lights, being touched by a stranger. I silently promise to give her a belly scratch when we get home. "Dwarf Burmese, almost five?" he asks.

I nod. The room has a cat stink and I don't know how seriously I can take a doctor named Gavin. I tell him how long it's been since she's eaten.

He looks at me above the rims of his glasses.

"And I woke up with her in my bed last night. Stretched out really straight. She's never done that before. I think she might be sick."

He forces her jaws open with a tongue depressor. Her sharp, backward-curving teeth are almost an inch long. It's weird seeing them in the light. It's like discovering your dad has a gun in his desk. The muscles in her jaw contract, trying to snap shut. Jasper is leaning against the doorframe staring at a poster of a cat tangled in a mess of computer wires. WAIT, I'LL FIX THIS, reads the caption.

"Was she next to you when you woke up?" Dr. Gavin asks. "Head to head, feet to tail?"

I nod. Maybe it's a common, easily fixable python problem.

He looks directly into my eyes the way I imagine a real doctor does when he tells you you're going to die. He has a single jubilant nose hair. "You can never be sure, and I don't want to worry you unnecessarily. But it sounds like she's planning to eat you."

Jasper laughs, then stops when he realizes Dr. Gavin is being serious. I take a step back. The fluorescent lights seem brighter. Voldemort slithers lazily. Her tail doesn't fit on the table. It twists in the air. At her widest, she's thick as a basketball.

"You have to understand, even domesticated pythons are wild animals," Dr. Gavin continues. "They might get used to humans, but they don't bond in the same way as a dog or a cat. And when they're planning to eat large prey, they void their stomachs and compare their size to make sure it's . . . feasible."

I've fed her religiously for four years. Mice first, then rats and rabbits. I give her a chicken once a month, and last Christmas a goose. I had to sit on the lid of the tank while it flapped and banged around. Hundreds and hundreds of dollars I spend to make her happy. I take another step back and bump into a weasel skeleton. There are all sorts of skeletons on the counter behind me: cat, raccoon, beaver.

"You aren't just a cat doctor, are you?" I ask. "I mean, you were trained with all animals?"

He laughs. "Yes, we're all regular fully trained doctors of veterinary medicine here. I wasn't around when they chose the name. And like I said, I can't be sure that's what your snake is planning, but it is the most likely explanation. Burmese like big prey."

He pats my shoulder. "It's really not that big a deal. You have a healthy snake. As soon as she realizes you're not realistic prey, she'll start eating again. Until then, make sure the lid on her tank is closed tight. I'd recommend putting something heavy on it, just in case. Snakes are escape artists."

Prey. I try to imagine what it would be like to be eaten. Would I wake halfway inside her, up to my waist? Or maybe just a foot in? Or all the way, in the dark, with digestive acids eating my flesh? The goose kept kicking for a full minute after she swallowed it. I watched the whole time.

THE THREE OF US sit on stools in Taco Del Sol, where I work, eating burritos I made them for free. I did some serious Googling when I got home from Cats on Broadway and I'm not the only Burmese owner with a stretched-out snake experience. Although usually it's when the snake is planning to eat the family dog.

"We should kill it," Jasper says.

"Or find it a better home," Nancy says. "In a sanctuary or something."

"There aren't any python sanctuaries in Montana," Jasper replies.

"I'm trying to be helpful. You know how much Derek loves his snake. He doesn't want to kill it. Don't be a dick."

"It wants to kill him."

They sound like my parents: *"Fine, let him keep the stupid snake, but don't you think he should have some friends? Play a sport? Like a normal kid?" "Leave him alone! He's just shy."* Jasper is in front of a Corona poster: beach, bikini, palm tree. His long rectangular head blocks almost the entire bottle. I'm glad he failed o-chem. He'd be a crap doctor.

"It doesn't want to kill Derek specifically," Nancy says. "It's just following its instincts. Don't start with your simplistic masculine bullshit. *Kill, kill, kill.* Like one of those Redoubt assholes."

She has some guacamole on her chin I want to lick off.

"All right, all right," he says, holding up his hands. "But I really do think we should get it out of the apartment. Maybe the pet store will take it back."

"It's a she," I say.

JASPER COMES INTO MY ROOM with a stack of chemistry textbooks. "I want them out of my sight," he says, putting them on the lid of Voldemort's tank. He pats me on the back, real friendly. I guess he feels bad. It's easy to take the high road when you're getting laid. I take the books off as soon as he leaves. I don't want the lid to collapse and crush her.

Most of me doesn't, anyway. Part of me wants to kill her.

"Think you're gonna eat me?" I whisper, squatting in front of her cage with the machete my dad got me in Costa Rica. I think I could chop her in half with one swing.

One really good swing.

I lean back against my bed and stretch my legs. My posters of deadly spiders (black widow, funnel, the wandering Brazilian) look especially deadly in the moonlight. A purple galaxy glows inside my bong. Harry Potter action figures are being overwhelmed by a swarm of orcs on my dresser. It's almost midnight. Nancy isn't staying over. She and Jasper murmured to each other for a long time and then she left. I'm out of weed.

"After all we've been through? All those nights when I told you about my life and my problems, you were planning to eat me? All the times I fed you, the toys I bought . . ." I gesture to Voldemort's rubber snake friends and the Hermione Granger doll. I'm sure there's a Shakespeare quote that sums up this kind of betrayal poetically, but all I can think to say is, "Bitch."

Her head is hidden inside the log. I can only see the lower two-thirds of her bunched against the glass like a large intestine. I tap the glass with the blade. "Look at me, bitch."

THE SHADOWS of passing cars roll across the ceiling. The red numbers on my clock increase and start over. I picture her slithering out of her tank, across the carpet, into my bed, her cool skin tightening around my throat. I get up and put the chemistry books back on the lid.

I HAVE THE NEXT DAY OFF and decide to go for a hike in the Rattlesnake Wilderness. Voldemort is asleep in her cage. The rat is sleeping, too, its little head on the partially eaten plastic leaf. I didn't sleep at all.

I try to walk or bike at least four miles a day to lose weight. I've gotten down from a forty waist to a thirty-eight. It's hot out. The few shredded clouds look like they're fleeing a massacre. I turn off the main trail to avoid the dog walkers, and head up Spring Gulch.

The trail follows Rattlesnake Creek through dense woods for a mile, then opens in a clearing below Scapegoat Ridge. I like it here. There's an apple tree a settler planted a hundred-and-some years ago. It's gnarled and wise and looks both out of place and completely at home. Strands of barbed wire are stapled to its trunk to keep bears away. Grass and mushrooms and flowers grow in the sunlight. Towering lodgepole pines surround the clearing. There's some kind of beetle killing the pines. The beetles used to die in the winters, but the winters aren't cold enough anymore. All the environmental studies majors are talking about it. No one knows what to do.

I sit beside a pale mushroom as big as a dinner plate.

I can't kill her. It would be like admitting I'm wrong about everything. My parents would be relieved. "Maybe now he'll find a girl," my dad would say. And how would I do it? Stop feeding her? Chop her up?

A couple on mountain bikes zip by. They throw me mud-spattered smiles. It's hard to keep doing things when you have to do them alone. I wonder if the settler who planted the apple tree was alone, or if he had a wife and kid. Maybe his wife wanted apples. My history professor said settlers often abandoned their families because they couldn't stand the stress of worrying about them in such wild country. It's one thing to live with the fear of getting scalped or eaten; it's another to imagine it happening to your kid.

I take out my pocketknife and cut away a chunk of bark at the base of the trunk. Then I start carving. After a few minutes, I lean back and admire my work: VOLDEMORT.

JASPER AND NANCY are in the living room watching the news. Violence has erupted again in Oregon, around Little Charbonneau, with new protests in Idaho and the Dakotas, and everybody watches now, with a feeling that something very bad is about to happen. The Redoubt is only a few hours from here, but from the look of the shouting, surging crowds it could be another country. Light from the TV flickers on Jasper's face. Nancy has one of her legs thrown over his, making them a single four-legged creature. I head for my room but he mutes the TV. "Derek," he says. "We need to talk to you."

I went six miles—all the way to the top of Scapegoat Ridge, plus the ride home. I want to take off my shirt and look in the mirror and see if there are any improvements. I'm hoping I can sleep. I flop down in the frayed recliner across from them.

"Nancy's roommate is moving out and we're moving in together. At her place," he says. His mustache is vaguely pubic. It vibrates when he speaks.

I want to close my eyes and ask if we can talk about all this in the morning and then never bring it up again. Jasper is my best and only friend. And Nancy—I haven't known her long, but they're the closest thing I have to family here. I don't want to be alone with my snake.

"I'm going to move my stuff over this weekend. I'll keep paying rent through the end of the month, of course."

"And we already put an ad on Craigslist for the room," Nancy says. "We'll show it, and if someone's good, we can all sit down together."

"I can get rid of her," I reply.

"It's not just the snake," he says. "We've been talking about moving in together for a while. Nancy's over here pretty much every night. She should be paying rent." He laughs weakly.

A protest leader is standing between her two sons on the TV, their rifles pointing to the sky, her mouth moving silently. I pick myself up out of the recliner, pretend it's no big deal. I turn toward my room. "Yeah, that makes sense. Congratulations. Let me know if you need help this weekend, with your bed or anything." I walk down the hall slowly, carefully.

"You can keep the TV and the couch, the stuff we split," he calls after me.

I LIE ON MY BED, looking at the stars on the ceiling. They don't form any meaningful constellations. It must've been a kid's room before I moved in. People have never liked me much. "If you're going to be fat, at least be fun," my dad said once.

Jasper's put up with me longer than anyone except my parents. Four years we've lived together. He helped me pass calculus. He did the dishes when I left them long enough. He was careful not to bring fatty foods home when I was on a diet. He never once acted like he felt sorry for me.

I spied on him and Nancy once. I heard them through the wall. We'd been to a party and I was drunk. Their door wasn't closed all the way. Nancy was on top and he had both his hands on her breasts. She was grinding against him. She grabbed the bed frame. He jostled her with his thighs. She threw her head back. The muscles in her shoulders stood out. Her ass was the whitest thing I've ever seen.

I've had sex with three girls. I had sex with one of them four times. But no girl has ever wanted to spend the day with me, or day after day. Let alone six months.

Voldemort slithers out of her log. She presses her head against the lid, where it meets the side of the tank. The gold parts of her skin have a caramel glow in the evening light. The markings on her face come together to form an arrow, pointing at me.

_____

BY SUNDAY, THE APARTMENT has tripled in size. I wander through the empty kitchen and living room. I find half a bottle of whiskey and a family-sized bag of Cheetos in the cupboard. I finish them both. Jasper's room is stripped. A few pieces of tape cling to the bare walls. There's a dusty square on the floor where his bed used to be. I try to imagine where his body went and where Nancy's body went. I wonder if they held on to each other all night, if people actually sleep like that. I wonder what their room, and bed, is like now.

She gave me a big Lysol-smelling hug before they left. "Come over all the time," she said.

"Really," Jasper added. "Don't hang out alone." I could tell he was happy to leave. He was tossing boxes around, practically skipping.

Voldemort is making the gentle rustling sounds that used to be a comfort. Barbed wire is duct-taped around the top of her tank. The steel barbs glitter. It looks like a concentration camp. The starving rat hardly moves.

"This is a lesson," I tell the air. Stop being fat and weird. Get rid of all the Harry Potter crap. Buy weights. Grow a beard. Do push-ups and watch football and smile whenever anybody says anything.

I've been telling myself to change for eighteen years, ever since Perry Macklin called me lardass and pinched me before nap time. But here I am, alone with my snake in a two-bedroom apartment at eleven-thirty on a Saturday night. The same as I've always been. She flicks her tongue at me.

I'm so tired my eyes hurt. I take the machete from the bed-side table and lie down. I show her the blade. One really good swing. In prehistoric times, the weakest members of the tribe got left behind for the predators. Too fat, too slow, too sick. The ones who couldn't carry their weight. The ones no one wanted around. They curled in hollows beneath the boundless maw of night, clutching sharp stones, listening to things move in the dark, waiting.

TOO MUCH LOVE

WHEN MY WIFE LEFT ME, I WENT BACK HOME TO IDAHO. TO the sagging double-wide on the bank of the Salmon River where my mother still lived, hoarding her Social Security checks, hissing and praying at the meth-heads and militiamen and philanderers who slunk through the Super 7 Motel next door. It was summer, thank Christ, but even with the windows open the dim, carpeted kitchen stank of menthols.

All the mills were closed, and no one was building houses. There was nothing I could do. I walked for miles along the river. Through downtown, past the baseball field and community center and the big bronze fish, all the way to the golf course. A battalion was camped on the fairway.

Thirteen-starred flags whipped above the holes and beer cans were strewn around the ragged tents. They'd commandeered the clubhouse as well; guards stood on either side of a sign:

RIGGINS

Capitol City of THE REDOUBT

"Wild and Free"

I nodded to them as I passed, not much caring about any of it. My wife's face on a chain saw loop through my head. And her body, my God. She'd moved to Nevada City with a weed farmer named R.W., which stood for nothing I could figure, doing things I could not bear to think about.

The air turned blustery in the afternoons. Sun-yellowed cottonwood leaves swirled on the water. I chewed Nicorette, toothpicks, the raw skin around my nails. The pop of rifle fire was the only thing that made me turn around.

My old friend Arn Campbell met me at the Lucky Diamond Casino. Standing hunched in the parking lot with a clove cigarette pinched between his fingers and an assault rifle strapped to his back. He looked like he was trying to find his last scrap of pride. Only thirty-two, his face was etched up like a cutting board.

"Come in with us," he said. "What have you got to lose?"

"You're a true believer now?" I asked. "Your blood for the tree of liberty?"

"This is your home, Les. They've gone too far."

"This isn't my home," I said. She was my home.

"Give it time." He looked into my bloodshot eyes, as if he thought he understood.

IN HER EARLY TWENTIES, my mother was the most beautiful girl in Idaho County. Miss Feed and Grain, 1974. She rode to the fair on the back of a tractor, waving to children in the street. Now her dry, wrinkled skin overhung her jowls. When she lit her menthols I was afraid it would catch. The whole husk burn away, leaving what? Brittle bones and organs coughing and cursing.

Still, she piled up her graying hair and crossed the street to Food Town. Found a basket and demanded a pound of potato salad from the girl behind the deli counter.

I was waiting for her on the porch. Hill kids floated by on rafts loaded with crates of ammunition. Drinking beers and eyeing me in that blank, sour, hill-kid way. I tried to figure where they were heading, and what kind of a wind it would take to blow them up. I was in the mood for fireworks. Mom raised the potato salad and pointed over them to the flat brown top of Patrick Butte. "Got a new shepherd up there. A Mexican boy. All the ladies organized a drive, as if he can't feed himself." She paused, suddenly wistful. "He slouches around like Charles Bronson. They're afraid he's going to leave."

Why he'd wanted to come in the first place, I couldn't understand.

Before we married, I took Jess up to see the sheep. Back

then there was no speed limit. We roared down the 95 at a 110 miles per hour, the future spread-eagled in front of us. A long, fine, fishing line of a woman. Coiled in my passenger seat. Cheeks red in the wind. All my CDs were scratched so we listened to parts of songs, singing along when we could.

The sheep ate down the knapweed while the shepherd and two collies watched from beside the Conestoga wagon. All three of them flat-heeled in the shade, the edges of the stretched canvas flapping lightly. "I didn't know that was still an option," Jess said, looking at the sheep, the dogs, the wagon.

"There are a lot of ways left to live," I said, meaning her and me. Meaning us.

Up there on the hilltop we were at the high-water line. Wave-forms marked the lip of the canyon. The great Lake Missoula flood—biggest in the world a hundred million years ago—busting loose its ice dam and crashing down to reshape Idaho's face. Mastodons and velociraptors pecking at the shore, some swept away. Spike-tentacled squid cruising the depths. Jess stood very straight. She searched the horizon with her light brown eyes. Purple-tinged clouds piled above the mountaintops and surged over our heads. Huge, silent airships, they blocked out the sun. She sucked in her breath.

I touched her cheek, afraid she might find something in the cumulus, the contrails.

She held my hand and leaned against my shoulder as we walked back down the grassy slope and across the railroad yard.

I felt like something then. Like I mattered.

Now she was with R.W. on his compound, trimming buds. Learning Spanish. Learning about wine. And the only good reason I could think of for joining the war was that I might get shot and not have to think about them anymore.

MOM HAD TWO television shows that she watched three times a day. Courtrooms; outrage. A man named Spud came around and put his feet in her lap. He was even older than she was. A retired trucker with a dented potato of a head and dark, tired little eyes. He grunted approvingly at each guilty verdict, and glared at me when I tried to switch to the news. Some men are born to hunker and lurk, like moles. If the feds busted through the door, I pictured him burrowing down between the cushions and disappearing for good.

I envied him, even as I imagined dragging him by the collar down to the river.

A woman. Nothing else matters.

I couldn't sleep. I couldn't eat.

Arn said I had given too much. "You've got to keep yourself inside," he said, scratching a crusted stain on his T-shirt, the AK leaning against his barstool. "Let it out a drop at a time, maybe one drop a year, so it'll last your whole life."

I stared into my beer. It was like getting breathing advice from a fish.

The waitresses all knew him. They called him "Lucky" and left little crumpled scraps of paper beside his beers. After they'd gone, he smoothed the scraps, his big, notched fingers deliberate as a priest's. Looking for a heart scrawled around a phone number or the red imprint of lipsticked lips. Each one was empty.

The waitresses giggled beneath the mirrored wall of liquor bottles. Their cheeks flushed. Emboldened by all the new men in town.

Time. It was grinding us to dust. Arn swept the papers onto the floor and looked down at the mess beside his boot. "Cunts," he whispered, so low he might not have said it at all.

Jess always said I had a tragic face. An actor in rehab, an actor on the curb. Construction, mill crews, landscaping—I was always the first to be let go. The boss never seemed to think I'd mind. Maybe that's why she married me. She was a psychic, a healer, a follower of Saint Jude. Lost causes all around. We didn't have a degree between us but she believed in the future. She kept crystals in the bathroom and a Tarot deck on the kitchen table. When the cards came out wrong she'd go quiet for days. Leave them faceup in a cross: cups and coins and Death himself blank-eyed while she moved carefully from the kitchen to the couch.

I started listing the places out loud where she and I spent the night—Deadwood, Sedona, Bend, Redding, Sioux Falls, Ontario, on and on—thinking if the number got high enough I might blow through the roof.

Arn turned away. The grid of the keno machine glowed blue on his face. Eighty chances. Eighty ways to lose. Fingers shaking, he slid in his last dollar, the one we were going to use for the tip.

Laughlin, Phoenix, San Bernardino. We were always on the move. She was against violence in all forms. She wore long green dresses. She used a cup to catch the ants that came in during the rain. Staggering across our warped linoleum floor, their black bodies heavy with moisture. I'd have stomped them, true. Scraped them off my boot on the same balcony where she set them free, her face pink and shimmering through the sliding glass door. Neon signs blurred along the freeway. Pine trees rattled in the storm. She was working at a club in Reno and I was looking, looking.

Broke in the sunlight, drinking water from a hose behind the bar, Arn told me a story about a man he'd known who married a girl with a withered hand. They kept going back and forth from Darby to Victor on account of he couldn't hold a job. He loved her too much. It made him lose track at the register, drop furniture, crash tractors. She got pregnant and when the baby came he left, believing himself unworthy of both mother and child. Drank himself to death without ever making it past Salmon.

"We drove there, too," I said. To the hot springs. Even faster, windows open, Jess's bare feet crossed on the dash. Her fingers tapping along with the music as she explained the rising signs. I leaned forward over the steering wheel and found that big, surging sky.

"Christ," Arn said. "You think you're the only one who's ever had a woman leave?"

In a past life, she claimed, she was a weaver. She saw the New World fall. Saw the burning of the books—that very moment when the lights went out. I often had no idea what was going through her mind. We made love standing up. Her head tipped back, the tendons in her neck like circus wires.

Arn leaned against the cinder-block wall holding the hose. Water dripped on his boot. His shadow stretched up to the roof. He was a tall man but hunched, skittish. Like a dog waiting to be kicked. He patted his pocket for a clove and the empty pack crumpled in on itself.

I asked him if he'd shot anyone.

He shook his head. "We just patrol the streets."

I pictured us side by side with AKs, day after day, walking the same empty six-block square where we'd grown up. Where we'd run with stick guns shooting imaginary cops. As if we hadn't grown up at all. But at least it would give me something to do.

Jess placed her foot on my forehead and stepped off into the sky. The last time I saw her, she was packing her bags in our apartment wearing rings on all ten of her fingers. Long, turquoise ovals. Her nails painted desert orange. She didn't even bother to take her shoes.

MOM THOUGHT I was home to stay. She cleared the magazines from my old room, and when Spud was out she listed her ailments: rheumatism, gout, cataracts. They sounded like dinosaurs lurching across the plain. Her voice softened, as if she could feel them bearing down.

"This country," she said. "I don't know what happened . . ."

She picked up a three-year-old copy of *Us Weekly* and held it in front of her like a prayer book. Thick purple veins twined around her knuckles. Forty years of carrying plates. Wiping tables. Scraping by. "You can't talk to anyone anymore."

"You'll be safe in town," I said. "With all the women and children."

But who knew? Growing up, I wouldn't have predicted firefights out past the fourteenth green.

It took her half an hour to unload the dishwasher. She held each glass up to the light, making sure it was still hers. The garden was weed swamped, the fence nearly swallowed, but she had Jesus for a saltshaker and a Harley-Davidson for pepper. She fit them together on the counter so the Son of God could ride.

I knew I'd leave the first chance I got. I couldn't take care of her; I couldn't even take care of myself.

The militia leaders held a press conference in front of the clubhouse, talking about how the country was rising up, from North Dakota to Arizona, but I hardly saw anything on the news. So long as the violence didn't spill over into Sun Valley or Phoenix, the people on the coasts didn't care. This rough strip of land could burn without even interrupting their vacations. The only rumor that scared me was about shutting down the roads. I couldn't stand the thought of getting stuck. Not with Mom, and Spud, and Arn.

My heart swelled across the country. If I'd had the money and the courage I'd have taken the bus. Twenty-five hours with my eyes bared, drinking coffee, eating teriyaki sticks.

Gotten off in Nevada City with a match. Said her name three times.

For six years we'd eaten together every night. So close I could watch the food go down her throat. Smell her tea tree oil shampoo. I washed the dishes while she paged through the *Good Housekeeping* magazines that were mistakenly delivered to our box. She read books about the landed, the genteel. She turned her long body in front of the mirror. She learned words in French and Japanese. Was she already planning her escape? Or did she think we'd go together—see the Alps, the nuclear craters? Drive across Tokyo in the middle of the night while she translated the neon signs?

I tried to picture myself navigating eight lanes of traffic under a Japanese moon. Could I have been that man? Not now. Probably not ever.

Maybe she'd been right.

I always said if I saw her with someone else I'd kill them both. Then I saw it—his face a polished tan knife through the window of Sushi Boat, her smile flicking on and off like a light—and I just stood there under a palm tree, my insides sliding down my leg.

I have the taste of ten thousand years' worth of dirt in my mouth. Sushi makes me retch.

Mom said what I needed was a job.

Spud said it was a younger girl. Maybe Asian. Not too pretty; not too bright.

I pictured bullets punching through the prefab walls.

———

THE FIRST AIR STRIKE took out the golf course—razing it to brown smoking dirt and killing forty men. The second blasted the community center into a tangled crater. We woke to the boom, felt a deep and terrible quaking, and then the sirens and screams.

In the morning, Spud and I took Mom to the see the crater. We walked down Main Street in the dawn quiet, one on either side, holding her elbows when she got unsteady. A chill mist clung to the buildings—Freedom Bank, Food Town, the Back Eddy Grill—with a chemical smell and black smoke in the distance. I saw Ridge Knotwell, the mayor, and old fat Sally Winder in her crossing guard vest, but no one said a word.

Lonesome joists lingered above the community center's rubble, as if waiting for permission to fall. No walls, though, nor part of a roof like you saw in old pictures of World War II. The hand-lettered sign lay among the torn concrete and beams: SENIOR NIGHT, SWING LESSONS. All the jamborees of days gone by. Looking at it, Mom's eyes welled up with tears. Remembering, I supposed, her Feed and Grain years. A ranch boy on her arm, the smell of her best perfume, all the warmth and possibility of a cornmeal-covered floor. She hadn't figured on ending up with Spud any more than I'd figured on ending up alone.

He spat nervously on the curb. Exposed in the sunlight, wanting to get back to his hole.

Mom wiped her eyes. She'd had her share of tragedies, but she hadn't prepared for her memories to get leveled by a drone.

THE MILITIA LEADERS made a big show with the coffins, lining them up outside the elementary school draped in thirteen-starred flags. They looked almost festive there, though in a timber box row the number was quite high. I counted back and forth. I knew some of the men inside. Assholes, even dead. I wondered who was making all the flags, and coffins, and if the time had come when I could walk into the bank and take what I could carry. But no one wanted to answer my kind of questions. Probably they were just ordering them on Amazon, along with the THREE PERCENT bumper stickers on their trucks.

General Diggs gave a eulogy on the concrete steps. She was pretty in a raw, mountainous kind of way—tall and haggard, with her brown hair pulled back above her defiant eyes, her sons on either side—standing high over everyone else. She said the dead had gone off to join her husband in martyrs' heaven, and her voice cracked when she spoke her familiar line, "An American, a mother, a widow . . ." There was no media left to record her speech. Just scared men with smartphones, beaming the pictures onto social media, where they were promptly taken down.

Arn was set to follow the generals into the mountains. "Phase Two," he called it, as if he were ready, though I could tell he was not. Winter was coming—not a pleasant time to be above the tree line. Particularly for a street-patrol man.

Mom and Spud decided to stay. Where else was there for them? They put a white flag in the front yard, like Switzerland, and spray-painted a big sign on the roof that read WE ARE OLD. I mouthed a silent prayer to the drone operator bunkered in Vegas or under a Colorado mountain, that he would see the sign, nod to himself, and nudge the joystick on.

It was time for me to go. East or west or north, as far as I could get. I knew where Mom hid her Social Security checks, and people had left behind plenty of cars I could steal. But I was gripped by something. It wasn't the community center, nor the men who'd died—I didn't care about them—but it reminded me of Jess. The way she'd blown me apart and stood back while my pieces landed in the dirt.

I had an old pistol in my duffel bag, and found my dad's Auto-5 shotgun in the shed where he'd left it when he'd gone.

"We might need that," Spud said.

"You've got the flag," I told him. And to my mom, "I'm going to see what I can do."

Her eyes showed pride then, for the first time in as long as I could remember. I tried to stamp that look into my mind and keep it there, in case I never saw her again.

ARN AND I drove in a line of trucks up toward He-Devil Peak, catching glimpses of the Snake River and Oregon to the east between the pines as his rusted Silverado coughed through the curves. There was a temporary cease-fire, time for all the peaceful folks to get out, but we were heading in the opposite direction. Past the abandoned ranger station and the shuttered gift shops of the ski village, all the way to Devil's Run Resort and the front line of the Redoubt.

A long traffic jam waited at a militia checkpoint in the dusk. We slowed and then stopped. The bed of the truck in front of us was piled with guns and mountain bikes, as if in an emergency the men inside could rip down the mountain on two wheels, bouncing over rocks and spraying machine gun fire. The evening sky was strangely yellow, like egg yolk, like something was burning. Sprawling condominiums had been left half built at the foot of the chairlift when the militia moved in. The foundations pronged out of the earth like fossils. ASPEN ACRES—FOR SALE! SKI-IN! the sign read, with LIVE FREE OR DIE spray-painted over it. Dark rocks jumbled the ridge, along with radio towers, their red lights blinking a mournful code. Arn and I were sharing a bottle of Rich & Rare. Throats burning, eyes watering, mad with the past.

I thought of getting out and running south. I could make it to Salt Lake City by Christmas, Nevada City in the new year. Show up gaunt and bearded on Jess's doorstep after crossing all those mountains and deserts. Or else send her some powder like anthrax in the mail and move on. Find a Mormon girl with lots of sisters. Settle down, build a house, become a God-fearing man.

Anything but this.

I craned my head around and looked back through the cab

window at the faint lights of Riggins. I tried to pick out my mother's trailer amid all the lonesome specks. Down along the river, where it had always been. Where I'd been leaving her since the first day I could.

Across the valley, Patrick Butte shone gold in the setting sun. I imagined the collie driving a milling cloud of sheep back toward the Conestoga wagon, where the shepherd Charles Bronson waited on the buckboard for my mother, young again, running up the hillside on her long legs. "He must get cold at night. All this way from home," I said.

"What?" Arn asked, his eyes on the road

"The Mexican boy."

"You've got to untwist yourself," Arn said. "It's too late for that crap now." He gestured at the shoulder. Men with guns lined the road, peering in at us, their padded vests packed with ammunition and protein bars. Stockpiling everything, knowing it would soon run out. Up past the checkpoint was a flurry of activity, crates being passed, orders shouted in the fading light. They were making barricades, bunkers, preparing for a winter war. He was right: I'd picked a side, and now the fear was setting in.

The moon was a frail little wafer behind the pink and purple clouds. A breeze came down and swung the chairs on the chairlift. The men along the shoulder coughed white jets of steam. Threatening even in their weakness. Cold seeped through the open window. I gripped the knees of my jeans. Dug my nails in. Thought of Jess and R.W. passing a joint in the California sunset, the tips of their fingers touching each time. Dumb, childlike smiles on their lips. The same country but another world.

Some of the skeletal condos had blue tarps wrapped around the joists, and generators and lights inside. Arn glared out at them with forced, furious triumph. "Rich pricks," he said, as if the owners were close enough to hear, tied to one of the remaining trees, getting what was coming to them. Getting theirs for all they'd taken from us.

My hands shook. My mouth was dry. I would've forgiven Jess in less time than it took to say the words, but she wouldn't even give me that. She'd started crying as soon as I raised my voice. Put her face in her hands. Said he owned a farm. Said the only reason she'd ever met him was to help me find a job.

Me, the weight around her ankles.

I called her names.

The breeze stung my cheeks. I cranked the window up. It was her fault. All of it. The cold, me being here, the entire country breaking apart. The Redoubt, the true West, where all the Indians were dead and we white men had finally gotten around to killing ourselves.

An owl hooted. Its shape moved blackly across the sky. I'd heard if you saw one in daylight it meant something precious was going to be taken from you. Luckily I didn't have much left. My inheritance was about to be turned to scrap. I began to cry.

Arn turned to me disbelievingly. He jerked his head at the men watching us outside and told me to cut it out. I refused, unable. He leaned over, whiskey on his breath, his face red and embarrassed, and hissed at me, calling me a fool, self-pitying, selfish.

"What kind of friend are you?" I asked through my tears.

He knotted his fingers in the front of my shirt. He shook me—my body limp as Jesus—and said it was time for me to stand up for something. He was sick of how I lived. Always passing through. Speaking only of myself. Expecting others to stick with me when I'd never stuck to anything. My mother . . . and there were times when he'd needed a friend. Weeks when the hours he'd slept could be counted on one hand.

"You didn't know her," I said. "You've never had a love like that."

"I knew her, you son of a bitch." He let loose of my shirt. His greased hair had sprung over his ears. "Her name was KaryAnn, and she left me on a bus full of Jesus freaks. She's got three boys now, and a place outside Spokane."

The blue of his eyes was so bright it hurt. He slicked down his hair, his big hands cupping around to the nape of his neck. Flashlight beams played across the windshield. KaryAnn. All I remembered of her was blond hair and the way he'd stood up straighter when she held his arm.

"Arn," I said.

But he shook his head, our suffering enough to fill the cab.

"We have to fight," he said. "They won't stop until they've run us out. It's all we've got left."

When we were kids, we'd played one-on-one for hours

in the schoolyard, banging the ball off the rusty orange rim while the river rushed by.

I'm sorry, Mom, that I turned out so poor. Maybe Arn was right, if I'd stood for something . . . or maybe now if Jess saw my flag-draped coffin on the news. Would she love me then? Was that what women wanted? To hold on to you while you held on to something else? I pictured her driving with the wind in her hair, an old song on the radio, cactus and crystals in the trunk. Sliding on, as if America were made of glass.

It was too late. There were the guns at my feet and the only comfort I could think of was to spread it around. I pictured R.W. in a prison camp, his legs shackled, his full name written out across his chest for all to see. Richard William. Ron Wayne. Some dumbass thing. I looked at Arn, still glaring at the line of bedraggled men along the road in the darkness, and I almost laughed. I'd never once picked a winning team. There was no reason to think I'd start now.

HARVEST

EVERY MORNING I LET CASS OUT TO WALK AMONG THE SILOS.
She blinks when I unbolt the blast door and heave it up,
revealing a bright circle of sky. Even in the bitter sleet of winter, she blinks, wonder lighting her sallow face from within.

I replace the sod over the door and go to sit in the wicker chair
on the porch of Lindeford's decaying farmhouse a few yards
away. The federal looters left the chair behind. They took or
smashed most everything else, and scrawled Traitor in red letters across the door. I have thought to wash it off, but its absence
might arouse suspicion. The time for bravery is long gone. Shards
of glass crunch beneath my boots. The seat cushion is frayed and
the wooden arms unraveling. The chair rasps, protesting my
weight. I set my rifle across my knees and watch Cass.

She walks stiffly at first, getting used to the soft ground and the open space. Her spread fingers test the dry, wheat-smelling air. The green dress she wears belonged to her mother. It fits her loosely, falling off one shoulder and then the other. Her legs are long pale bones, slightly bowed, with red knobby knees. They make her clumsy, and I worry that she will be too frail to bear many children.

The yellow prairie blankets the horizon, broken only by her thin receding figure and the three silos. From a distance, the silos look like the hilts of swords driven into the earth. She brushes her fingers along the corrugated steel sides. She stops, kicks the steel, and stands back, listening.

DUCKLINGS FOLLOW THEIR MOTHER through the shallows of the pond behind the farmhouse. Eleven tufts of straw-colored fuzz, paddling in a line. Cass and I leave our clothes hidden in the reeds on the shore. I follow her into the cold murky water holding a bar of soap. The skin on her back is white as paper. She insists that I be very quiet as I bathe her, so as not to disturb the ducklings. It is hard for me. I treasure these moments, I have for four years: the splashing, the excitement, untangling her hair. She wriggles in my hands like a fish.

"TODAY AT LAST the nation rebuilds. Today at last the nation rebuilds. Today at last . . ." the federal propaganda repeats, an endless loop. A lie. I know patriots are still holding the

Redoubt. But here in the Dakotas, the battle is long lost. Cass sits cross-legged on the floor, her back straight, her hair in two wet braids. Her cheeks are still flushed from the fresh air, and to add to their color she has dabbed red paint beneath her eyes. She is beautiful in her ungainly way. I let her listen for as long as she wants.

"That's us," I tell her, turning their lies against them. "Rebuilding."

She nods but she does not speak. She says less and less as she ages. She is twelve now, almost thirteen. Her fingers are red with paint. She spends hours in front of the mirror, adjusting herself. Perhaps it is part of growing up. I was selfish, too, in my youth.

The toys I made for her are balanced on the shelf above our bed. A twig-and-twine giraffe. A carved rubber elephant. Knitting needles and a straw doll with a red bow around its neck. She used to carry them from corner to corner: elephant pursuing giraffe, giraffe pursuing doll, doll wielding needles.

I turn the radio off and lock it in the safe. For lunch, we have canned pineapple, popcorn, and tuna. All her favorites.

ELM TREES are painted on the walls of the bunker, and the couch is white with black spots, like a cow. The main room is a hexagon with a small kitchen and bathroom attached. We named each corner: one is the Library, another the Nook, a third Hollywood, where the mirror is. We keep art supplies and a little pot of clay in the drawer beneath the bed.

On special occasions—birthdays, holidays, stormy nights —I use the projector to display a crackling fire on the tall white dresser opposite the couch. The dresser is ancient, an heirloom built by Lindeford's great-grandfather. It stands unsteadily on four short legs. The subbasement is packed with canned food, ammunition, and gasoline for the generator. The Pantry, we call it.

In the evening, we do a progression of exercises I learned in the field hospital after the Fargo Offensive. Leg lifts, crunches, twists for the back. I had shrapnel in my legs, and for a time they were worried that I would never walk again. Lindeford was on the cot beside mine, his fractured skull swaddled in bandages. All night he mumbled, delirious, about his beautiful wife and daughter, their home, and the bunker he had made for them.

Cass arches her back, her arms over her head, looking at the wall behind her. I support her hips with my hands. The single bulb turns her pale skin gold. I swore to protect her, and I will. I squeeze her gently. Perhaps in another time she could have been a dancer.

When she undresses for bed, I check her undergarments. Tall as she has become, there is still no blood.

THE ANTELOPE COME in September. Cass sees them first. She gasps, on the ladder halfway out of the bunker. The herd is way off across the prairie, miles and miles away. They are the size of beetles.

I remember a story Lindeford told me about a dog he had

as a boy. The dog ran away one morning. Lindeford and his family watched it for three days, growing smaller and smaller, and then his dad drove out in his pickup and brought it home. "Nothing can run away on that prairie," Lindeford finished. "There's nowhere to go."

Cass begs me not to go after the antelope. She is a gentle girl, and I appreciate her delicate nature, but we need the meat. She needs it, for her spirit and her hips. I lock her in the bunker and set off, staying downwind, moving as fast as I can on my damaged legs.

Their hides are the color of sunset. I lie on my belly, the rifle's barrel steadied on a hillock between two stunted clumps of brush. The animals twitch even when they are standing still. Their black noses spit white clouds and their haunches tremble. My first shot is bad. It clips a female and the herd scatters, bounding full speed across the grassy distance. I shift the barrel, exhale, and squeeze again. A buck drops.

It is past midnight when I finally arrive home, a skin full of meat slung over my shoulder. Cass begins to cry when she sees my blood-slick boots on the ladder.

THE NEXT DAY, I prepare to track the injured female. Cass is still in bed, wrapped in the sky-blue comforter. She refused the meat I cooked her for breakfast, and now she refuses to kiss me goodbye. A years-old fashion magazine lies beside her in the bed. She has paged through it so many times the cover is falling off.

The blood trail leads east, toward Devils Lake. I follow it across the flat yellow ground, keeping low, with one eye to the south, where the road is. I have not seen a federal patrol out this way in years, but there is no sense in being reckless.

Miles pass beneath my feet. Unchanging miles of scrub brush and abandoned wheat fields gone to seed. Golden clouds of chaff swirl above the stalks. Gray clouds unfurl low in the sky. The drops of blood grow faint and then disappear. The antelope is gone, swallowed by the empty prairie.

Tired and irritated, I return home, wondering if Lindeford lied about the dog.

I sense trouble as soon as I reach the silos. Vibrations. A wrongness in the air. I creep through the grass to the farmhouse and lay my ear on the cool prickly ground. I hear a faint murmur inside the bunker. Voices. My body goes cold. I crack the rifle's bolt, making sure the chamber is full. No one knows we are out here. They will hang me if I am caught, armistice be damned. But I will not leave her. I have worked too hard, waited too long.

The sod over the hatch seems undisturbed. Its edges are barely distinguishable from the grass around it. I order my hands to stop shaking and unlock the door. My rifle goes in first.

Cass is on the bed with the radio. The announcer is babbling about a sunny day in Minneapolis, no rain at all in the forecast. His strident, chirpy voice cuts away to a pop song about unity and a strong central government. Cass freezes when she sees me.

"Turn it off."

———

THE FARM WAS LOOTED when I found it: the windows broken, beer cans and bullet casings scattered in the grass. Graffiti covered the walls: TRAITOR, WHORE, STUPID AND DEAD— the old federal joke. It was hard to tell who was who in those final days. General Jensen had emptied the prisons during his retreat and all sorts of men, from both sides, were laying waste to the prairie.

Cass's mother's corpse was splayed halfway off the bed in the upstairs bedroom, stripped and bruised. The blood around her lips was not yet dry, and I could tell she had been beautiful. Her hips, in particular, were shapely. Lindeford had been a fortunate man. My heart heavy, preparing for a life of solitary confinement beneath the ground, I searched the house for the girl. I was sure I would find her in some horrible, mutilated state. I even checked the oven. But I found nothing, and a shred of hope returned.

I wrapped her mother's body in a sheet and carried it out to the middle silo. I was half starved, too tired to dig a grave, so I brought it inside, covered it in hay, said a few words about the heel of tyranny, and drove a nail through the lock in the door. Then I sat with my back against the corrugated steel as dusk painted the sky. I did not know the exact location of the bunker, only that it was in the yard, near the house. Night fell and the hours dragged on. I drifted in and out of sleep, starting at the tremble of every shadow.

In the morning, as the first rays of sunlight lit the tops of the wheat, a patch of the yard began to move. Jolted awake, I held my breath. It twitched and then heaved up, followed by a small hand.

I RETURN THE RADIO to the safe, setting it on top of my enlistment papers. The red seals of the Northern Liberty Militia and the Order of the Oathkeepers are stamped on each page, along with the motto "Wild and Free." I remember the day they were given to me, the proudest of my life: in a long line of recruits before the capitol tent in Riggins, swearing allegiance to the Constitution before Generals Diggs and Jensen, the thirteen-starred flag of the original colonies flying overhead. Lindeford's ring gleams in the back corner of the safe. Cass knows that the radio is forbidden when I am gone. She has grown sly, deceitful. It pains me, after all that I have done for her. I do not know how to reset the combination. Anger heats my chest.

She is rigid on the bed, eyes wide, waiting. Her slight new chest rises and falls. Her foolishness, like her mother's, will get her killed. I slap her. She quivers but she does not cry. I slap her again, harder. Her cheek turns crimson and she sucks in air. I forbid her to leave the bunker for a month. I drag her by the arm into the bathroom to sleep on the cold concrete.

"I know it's hard for you to understand, you were so young," I say through the door. "But what you heard are lies. They will kill you if they find you. Torture you and kill you, like they did your parents."

CASS SPENDS MOST of the next three days in Hollywood, with her back to me, drawing dark, indecipherable landscapes. I do not leave the bunker. I watch her reflection. The outline of her once-plump lower lip has hardened and I catch her looking at me with a frightening coldness. A bruise colors her cheekbone. I explain that I am only trying to protect her.

Silent, hunched, she draws.

When she is a woman, she will understand. She will come to appreciate all that I have done for her. The time cannot come soon enough. I make her stand so I can check her underwear. Still there is no blood.

The longer the season the richer the harvest, I remind myself.

A storm rolls in from the west and I turn on the fire and carry her into the Nook. Limp, she does not struggle. We listen to the muffled thunder and rain. The storms are stronger now than when I was a boy, and it is nice being inside the bunker. A reminder of how safe we are, how insulated, here in our little world. Even as everything has fallen apart above. I comb and braid her hair, trying to make peace. The orange flames lick the face of the dresser. I tell her about the Battle of Grand Forks: the way the line held even after our captain had fled, and the three men I saved by kicking a grenade out of our trench. I claim that one of the men was her father, though I had not yet met him. I massage the nape of her neck. Her muscles are tight, unyielding.

After she goes to sleep, I open her drawing pad. Tipping the pages right and left, I realize that she has been drawing cities. Skyscrapers stacked like black teeth gnawing at the sky. I tear them up and drop the pieces into the trash. The smell of old tuna wafts out. The air in the bunker suddenly feels stale, pressing down on me.

I lean over our bed, inhaling her sweet young night-scent. The lines of her face are softened by sleep. Her body is hardly wider than my outspread hand. I gently pinch her nostrils until she twitches and her eyes pop open.

"I love you," I whisper.

ON THE FOURTH DAY, I leave the bunker to hunt. I am reluctant to go. There is still a darkness in Cass, a rebellion, but winter is coming and the chances for meat are rare. I put the radio in my pack along with a bottle of water, extra ammunition, and a protein bar.

The sky is wrenchingly blue. Not a cloud. Not a speck of dust. It is the kind of late autumn day that makes me afraid of death. Afraid to ever leave a world so beautiful, even if the federals did win.

It is not wrong that I should want some part of myself to carry on.

Grouse are roosting in a stand of willows by Burley Creek. I flush them out. They roar into the air, an explosion of feathers that drowns out the three rifle shots. I look toward the distant dirt road, making sure the noise has not drawn any attention. Then, humming an old freedom song, I clean the birds and string them on a stick.

I sit on a rock beside the creek. I finger the small Constitution in my shirt pocket. Its pages are worn soft. I know many of the words by heart. I take off my boots and let the cold water run over my feet. My toes are more gnarled than I remembered, with long yellow nails. I am growing old. The dirt between them washes away and the fine hairs on the knuckles ripple like reeds.

IT WAS A FAVOR that I did for Lindeford. The bullet had caught him in the stomach and he was suffering. We were overrun. There was no point in staying to die like a fool, and I could not just leave him there. I had heard what the federals did to the survivors at Bismarck. Impaled, their naked flesh peeling in the sun.

He was propped between the roots of a maple at the end of the cul-de-sac we had been defending. A mortar had blown off the roof of the house behind us, and in the open maw of the second story a wooden crib was visible, full of plaster and debris. Blood and sweat glistened on Lindeford's contorted face. I knelt beside him and swore that I'd look after his wife and daughter. I will not leave them, I told him. You have my word.

I took his wedding ring so they would know me as a friend. Then, with a single shot, I relieved him of his misery.

CASS IS SITTING on the bed, her back against the wall, her legs crossed, when I return home. Her hair is twisted on top of her head in a bun, and she is wearing a short black skirt that I have not seen very often. She has a blank, stunned look, like she just glimpsed the underworld.

The air smells fresh, lemony. She has been cleaning. I fear some new disobedience. "What's wrong?" I ask.

She points to the floor.

A pair of her underwear lies crumpled in front of the dresser. I go toward it and she rises to join me. Red spots stain the white fabric, like rose petals on fresh snow. I blink, standing over it, gratefulness and joy stretching my rib cage. "My sweet girl."

A warm glow fills the bunker. I imagine a cradle beside the bed, the branches of the largest elm spreading above it. A mobile of carved ducklings hanging from the ceiling. I see our family: Cass beside me, babies in both arms, proud northern stock, rebuilding . . .

A nervous sweat dampens my palms. It has been so long. She is so slight, so beautiful. I will be gentle at first, and slow. I will give her her father's ring.

I kneel and rub the blood between my fingers. It is fresh and sticky and warm. I look up, hoping to catch her in my arms. Both her hands are wrapped around the back of the dresser. Her young face is hard as stone. I do not understand. She twists with all her strength, her whole body pivoting as she throws the dresser down.

I raise my hands to stop the falling shadow.

THE AIR IS SO BLACK that at first I do not know if I am awake or dead. I taste blood. I reach up to rub my eyes. An intense, frightening pain blooms in my arm. I gasp and twist. I do not touch it because I know I would feel the broken bone.

"Cass!" I yell, kicking my legs, trying to clear my throbbing head. A can falls onto my thigh. It is only an inch high, but as wide as any other can. Tuna. I am in the Pantry. All around me are cans. Stacks and stacks of them, packed into the darkness.

I bump my head on the ceiling. Nausea floods my stomach. I try to be calm, make myself breathe. The ceiling is so low I can hardly crawl. Pain rolls over me, recedes, then returns. If she dragged me down here, I must be near the hatch. I need a sling, bandages. I had no idea she was so strong.

"Why would you do this?" My voice disappears in the inky air.

With my right hand, I search the concrete ceiling for the hinges. I scrape along, blind as death. It is hard to breathe. I wonder if my lungs are damaged, or if there is not enough oxygen. I am going to suffocate; I am buried alive. The two thoughts arrive in unison, accompanied by the memory of Cass in the pond, laughing and squirming. I scream her name again. "Please."

There is no answer. Not a single footstep above me.

It seems like hours in the darkness before I find the rounded metal hinge. I push against the wood. The hatch has no lock, but there is something heavy on it. The dresser, probably, and who knows what else. Maybe everything: the bed, the fridge, the mirror, her toys. The whole world we made together. I push with all my strength. I push until the pain turns white-hot and all I can do is lie on my back and gasp for breath.

WHERE ARE YOU? Cass, my sweet, cruel girl.

I have no idea how much time has passed, or when exactly I will die. I lie in the darkness. I sweat and rage and picture her. I see her on the plain, growing smaller and smaller, a bag of provisions slung over her shoulder, her slight frame bent against the wind. I see her in an eastern city, beneath the vaulted pillars of glass, a thousand shoulders bumping her as she stares up at the top floors, the rich men's offices and penthouses. Who will find her there? She is still but a child. I think of men so crude and vile that I pound my fist against the ceiling until the shelves around me rattle and more cans fall to earth.

In gentler moments, when I assume it is dusk though I have no way of knowing, my anger calms and I see her in the countryside. In a small house not far from here, on the edge of Devils Lake. A house with many windows, where she can look out at the boundless prairie and the distant place where the yellow land meets the blue sky. Where her parents' farmhouse still stands, and where, below, I wait for her.

THE REDOUBT

MERCY GASPED IN PAIN AS WE BUMPED OVER THE BRANCHES of the lightning-struck tree that marked the border at Wallowa Pass. The Redoubt behind us, lawful states ahead. Her knuckles dug into my ribs; her fingers knotted the sides of my shirt. The arrow that ran through her midsection was pressed against my waist. Her face, when I turned, was as pale as the spring snow drifted on the shoulder.

"Don't stop," she said.

The four-wheeler growled beneath us, heavy tires churning. An orange scrap of cloth hung like a failed totem from the tree's blackened roots. Above, lift chairs swung silently in the abandoned ski resort. I listened for hoofbeats, engines, a voice disguised as a birdcall.

Down the mountain, meltwater threaded through canyons and gullies and cracks in the road. Switchgrass grew between patches of snow. Small purple flowers strained toward the sun. I downshifted to neutral, hoping to save what little gas we had left. My arm brushed the red-painted feathers of the two arrows jutting from my thigh. The four-wheeler picked up speed. The pain had ebbed to a dull, sickening ache.

Rain began to fall. Cedar trunks gleamed and their sweet smell filled the air. Clouds sank around us, ghostly fingers reaching between the branches. We surprised a herd of mule deer grazing in a foggy swale. They looked up, froze, and then ran, their white hindquarters disappearing into the trees. I squinted to see the road. Mercy huddled against my back.

Down we plunged, holding tight to the winding road, the mountainside falling off to the right, our bodies angled forward, rain in our eyes. My hands went numb. The motor choked, came back to life. Mercy pressed her face into my shoulder. She spoke softly: praying, cursing.

THE LOCHSA LODGE stood at the end of the dirt road beside the river. Mercy lifted her head. The storm had passed. The western horizon was streaked violet, pink, and orange, as if paint had spilled from the mountaintops.

Dusk. I was amazed to be alive.

A bleached school bus rested in the mud in front of the lodge, only the tops of its tires revealed. I parked beside it and cut the engine. "Beware of dog," Mercy said, reading the words painted in black on the side. A white s was scratched at the end. We sat still for a moment, searching the shadows for yellow eyes, a rustling chain. Then, slowly, pain jolting up my thigh, I stood.

A small flower of blood bloomed around the arrow's shaft on Mercy's dress. The obsidian tip gleamed in the twilight before her. Mud flecked her cheeks; her eyes were tired, dazed. She held my arm and together we limped around the bus to the lodge.

The log walls were gold in the fading light. Drops of water fell on the rusted Browning mounted on the porch. They slid off the barrel and down the silver chain of ammunition. Mercy stopped, staring at the American flag nailed like a warning beside the door. The rain shone in her hair. I touched her hip, and we went inside.

The old innkeeper coughed, eyes watering, behind the desk. His whole body shook. He buried his gray beard in his elbow. A cigarette smoked in the bear-paw ashtray beside him. The rest of the bear crouched in the corner—a poorly taxidermied mess—its remaining paw stretched toward the door. Hacking, the innkeeper spat into a milk jug. "Christ Jesus." He wiped his mouth on the sleeve of his coat and stared at Mercy. "You come over the mountain?"

I nodded.

His eyes, blue and bloodshot, turned to my face. "Not many that make it anymore."

"A room," I said.

He watched me, unmoving, until I set a small gold ring on the desk.

"Names," he said, sweeping it into his palm.

"Lyle and Shannon Reeves."

He held the ring up to the light and a crooked smile formed on his lips. "Honeymoon?"

I stared at him blankly, then nodded. Mercy leaned against me.

"Newlyweds from traitor country." He dropped the ring into a metal box full of other jewelry, as well as coins and bills, and spread his arms, taking in the dark lobby, the suffering bear. "Welcome to civilization."

"We won't be staying long," I said.

"Expect not." He took down the last key on the left and unfolded his body from the stool. "You'll be wanting a cabin. For the privacy." He grinned again, picked up his cigarette, and came slowly out from behind the desk, smoke drifting over his head.

We followed him down the creaking porch past the numbered doors of the main lodge. The distant river gleamed like a copper wire in the sunset. He wheezed down the steps into the ragged field that stretched to the water. Half-deflated balls and chewed bones lay in the grass. Large gray shapes were twisted together in the corner of the kennel along the far side. They rose, untangling themselves into the looming forms of Dobermans that pressed their jaws against the chain-link.

"I had a wife once, too," the innkeeper said. "Nothing but pain in it." He paused. "How old are you kids, anyway?"

Silently, we followed.

The cabin was a single block of rough-hewn logs on the riverbank. I looked at the surrounding trees. I'd expected everything to be different once we escaped the Redoubt, as if the dominion of President and governors and sheriffs would extend even to tree branches. But the pines were as wild-reaching as ever. Sticks tumbled past in the high, mud-brown water. Moss hung from the edges of the cabin's roof. The walls were gray with age, as if it had been there long before the rest of the lodge. Holding my leg, I followed Mercy inside.

A rotten smell filled the room. The innkeeper set the key on the dresser. He paused in the doorway, his large face mottled with shadow, and looked at the arrows in my thigh. "I've seen them who go both ways," he said. "And I've seen it end well and I've seen it end bad, but there are pliers in the drawer if you need." He turned to Mercy in the half-light. The arrow pierced her side just above the kidney. "That one you might best leave alone."

THE BRASS BED frame curled and gleamed like something I imagined in a mansion. I sat on the squeaking edge. My stomach went loose at the sight of the two shafts sprouting from the bloodstained canvas of my pants. The tips were lodged deep in the muscle. The red-painted feathers trembled with my pulse.

I'd been lucky, we both had, but it didn't feel that way.

Mercy stood silhouetted in the window, looking north up the river to the mist rolling down the mountainside. Beech trees trembled in the wind; their white branches moaned like loons. Her arrow was longer than mine. Nearly three feet of carved cedar painted black, a bit of copper in the nock. A sniper's arrow. A taker of lives, greatly prized in the Redoubt, where bullets were more valuable than gold.

She moved into the small kitchen. Her hair fell across her cheek as she bent over the drawer. She found the pliers: steel, with serrated teeth and black rubber grips. She lifted them and held them delicately, a hand on each handle, opening and closing the steel mouth. "Shannon Reeves," she said. "From traitor country."

"We're alive."

She stared at the pliers, waiting for me to go on. I pushed myself up and limped across the space between us. I faced her side so the shafts in my thigh stood out behind her and formed a floating crucifix with the shaft beneath her ribs. I lowered my forehead to her ear, smelling sweat. The knees of her dress were dirt-stained. Dried blood flecked her feet. She'd fallen when the arrow hit, but before I could even go to her she'd been up again, running.

IT WAS FULL DARK when I limped back across the field. Like a fool, I'd left our bag, with what little food we had, strung to the back of the four-wheeler. The Dobermans rose and followed me to the edge of the kennel. Collarless, like wraiths in the dark, they didn't make a sound. I gathered my damp shirt around me. A cold slice of moon glowed above the mountain's snowy peak.

The innkeeper and three other men were playing cards around an oil lamp in the office. They heard my feet on the gravel and every head upturned. The game froze, cards and money poised inches above the table as they stared out into the night.

I ducked my head.

"Just the boy," the innkeeper said, his voice carrying through the open window.

The seat of the four-wheeler was still warm. Unscrewing the gas cap, I checked the level with a wire. Two gallons, maybe less. My father had often spoken of the cities on the coast, San Francisco and Seattle, millions of people living together in skyscrapers, crossing bridges built over the sea. Places where we might disappear. I untied the bag and slung it over my shoulder.

The decrepit bus sank and rusted in the dark. Far off, a coyote yipped. Crickets answered, their sawing bows the breath of night.

JUST BEFORE DAWN, our arrows tangled together and I woke gasping in pain. Warm blood ran down my thigh. I could hardly breathe. I thought of my parents, my brother, our farm. Unable to stop myself, I began to cry.

Mercy laid her palm on my cheek. She undid her dress and

coiled her body around mine. She kissed my eyelids and held my face until the roar of the river overtook the sound.

Cold air seeped through the windows. I pulled her close. My lips found her neck, her smell. I tasted sweat. Obsidian slid across my side and nicked up my ribs. Her legs locked around my waist. I breathed her name in quick, light shivers.

She pushed herself up, wincing and arching her back so it touched the shafts that rose stinging from my thigh. Her breasts were ghostly in the moonlight. Their paleness frightening, as if the spark that lit her had burned too bright. Her stomach taut to the lines of her pelvis. Her face locked in a grimace of pleasure and pain. She fell forward, her hair in my face, cheek pressed to my ear. Fire coursed down my leg and lifted my spine from the mattress. I wrapped my arms around her. She made a low, catching sound. I felt myself being pulled upward; she was all I had left. The arrow feathers were like some strange flower growing from her spine.

THE DRY CRACK of the Browning shook me awake. Mercy was already out the door, wrapped in a sheet. A storm of barking rose from the kennel. I swung my legs off the bed, gritting with pain when they hit the floor, and followed her, naked as the sunlight. Insects and birds flitted away through the branches. She crouched at the edge of the trees, peering out.

The innkeeper whooped and coughed behind the Browning. Smoke drifted from the chamber. "Goddamn!" he yelled, and coughed mightily.

Mule deer were heaped among the tomato vines and carrot tops in the garden. The force of the bullets had flipped them over. Their hooves stuck up akimbo and two still gently fled through the morning air. In the kennel, the dogs were in a frenzy. They hurled themselves against the chain-link, crashing and sliding down, then scrambling back up.

"That's right, boys," the innkeeper said, leaving the gun. "Breakfast!"

He paused on the top step and looked our way. I pressed myself against the papery bark. Mercy stood, turned, and walked back to the cabin, the sheet trailing behind her like a wedding gown.

"THEY HAVE TO come out," I said.

"Constance lived for twelve years with an arrow through her gut," Mercy answered. She was organizing our belongings on the table: dried beef, apples, a flashlight, her knife. "She only died when she tried to have a baby."

I shook my head, touching the fletching. The barred feathers were split along the quill and tied with sinew. The outer edge was rough when I stroked down, then smooth going up, like a dog's fur. White pus floated below the surface of the scabs.

I braced my feet against the side of the bed. "It won't get any easier."

"You'll bleed," Mercy said.

I seized the first shaft with both hands and took a deep

breath. Midday sun streamed through the window. Birds called back and forth. I squeezed my eyes shut and yanked. The arrow didn't move but such a pain shot through my leg that I fell forward, sweat stinging my lips. Blood oozed through the pus. I was shaking. I thought I might vomit.

Mercy crossed the room and took my arm. "You can't. They're in the bone."

I shook her hand off and hobbled outside. The innkeeper was standing by the kennel with a bucket of bloody meat, passing strips through the chain-link, speaking to each dog by name. I fell back against the outer logs of the cabin. I cursed, looked at the branches and the ruthless blue sky, gripped the arrow, and prepared to yank again.

"For Christ's sake, boy, use the pliers, at least," the innkeeper called. He slapped a mosquito off his neck and set the bucket down. "They have to come out straight, clean."

The dogs' tongues lolled eagerly. They pawed the wet ground. I wished for a gun, a bow. I'd take everything he had.

"Now get on inside," he said. "I'm going to let them run."

THAT NIGHT, a group of federal soldiers set up camp in the field. They built a huge bonfire and roasted two deer on spits. They lay their guns in a circle around them. Sparks leapt to the darkening sky. The smell of cooking meat filled the air. Their dirt bikes lined the gravel in front of the lodge. They shouted and laughed and drank from battered metal cups.

I sat on the cabin's small porch with my back against the

doorframe and my legs straight out in front of me, trying not to look at the shafts jutting from my thigh.

One of the soldiers walked near, his arms full of firewood. His sandy hair was greased back from his forehead and his young face shone with sweat. "Christ, look at that," he said. "Right skewered."

I flicked a blade of grass off my wrist.

"When they get you?"

"Yesterday."

"Hell, we've a doctor who can take a look. Plenty of fresh meat, too." He shifted his weight, hefting the bundle of sticks up to his chin. His face was familiar: blond whiskers, blunt chin, greenish eyes. He looked like my brother. I remembered the clearing behind our farm where we'd played, and the bear that had come to scratch its back on the bark of a leaning pine. A million miles from here, and the mutilated corpse in the lobby.

"Thank you," I said.

THE VOICES RISING above the flames quieted when we approached. A short stout man with a bald eagle stitched on the breast of his leather coat stepped forward. Reddish sideburns framed his face. The skin around his lips was carefully shorn and the lips themselves were plump and moist, as if he'd once been a taster of fine foods.

"Hear you came over the mountain." He handed me a cup filled to the brim with whiskey. "That's reason enough to drink."

He gave another cup to Mercy. She took it and held it between her hands, standing back from the circle of men. Their eyes glanced off her and came quickly back. The doctor motioned for me to sit and knelt beside me, unpinning the place where I'd sawed my pants apart. His eyes sparkled as he looked down at my thigh. The hair above my knee was clotted with blood, the skin beneath it purple. "Did they come in the evening?" he asked. "Right when you were about to eat?" He shook his head. "The savages."

A silver lancet appeared from the pocket of his coat. I was afraid he was mad, some perverse field medic prone to creative procedures, but it was all I could hope for at the edge of two worlds. The orange sun lay half swallowed by the western hills. The Dobermans were up at the chain-link, staring at the slowly revolving deer on the spit. He poked the wound. I flinched. Pus leaked out and ran down my leg.

"Can you get them out?" I asked, my voice cracking.

He poured clear alcohol onto a rag. "Outside of John Day, I met a man with an arrow through his skull. Just like one of these, except here"—he pointed to his temple—"and here"—out the other side. "It gave him visions. For a bottle of whiskey, he'd tell you where you were going to die. Breathe, now."

He pressed the rag to my thigh.

The shock of pain sent my spine twisting away from itself, each vertebra trying to flee. I bit down so hard I was afraid my teeth would break. The soldiers watched, their eyes tired and gleaming, grease in their beards, cheeks flushed with drink. Small radios sat beside them in the dirt. One of them crackled and every man turned to listen, then looked up as the shadow of a drone passed far overhead. I sank to my elbows, fighting back tears.

The doctor smiled. His eyes were faded gray, like trout left too long in the sun. "Saskatchewan, he told me. I don't know if it was worth the whiskey, but I keep to the south." He clasped the near shaft with his thumb and forefinger and moved it from side to side, sending fresh waves of pain up my back. "That's the problem with youth: your body heals so fast. They've fused to the bone."

"Can you get them out?" I asked again.

He nodded. "But eat first. You'll need your strength. And tell us of the Redoubt. Many of these men have never seen it." The chewing mouths slowed and their eyes darted from Mercy to me.

My cup was refilled and they cut a shank from the deer and passed it around. Mercy sat behind me, her knees at her chin, eating quickly, voraciously. After the pain lost its sharpness, I, too, ate and drank, and a warm drowsiness fell over me. For a moment I felt safe. My tongue loosened. I told them of the bands that roamed from Garden Valley to White Bird, driving herds of cattle ten-thousand-head strong, bunkering in the mountains, warring over remaining weapons and supplies. The looted towns, debris mounded into pyramids that could be seen for miles across the plains. And the few surviving loyalist farmers, like my father, who'd made their own tenuous peace.

The sun disappeared and the soldiers' faces reddened in the firelight. They listened and nodded and ate. Other voices piped up, speaking of battles along the Wallowa Line, ambushes in the night. Occasionally a radio crackled and the man beside it picked it up and held it to his ear.

Silence fell, and then the doctor clapped me on the back. His mood jovial, unflagging, yet tinged with a sourness I couldn't place, like copper on the tongue. He told me his father wasn't so different from mine. "Brave fools. They think they'll save this country yet." He poured me more whiskey and turned to Mercy. "And you, what do you have to say of your people?"

She stared at him, holding the last of the venison, her lips shining with grease.

"Come, now, if you don't tell it, what will we believe?" He looked at the young men and boys around him, concern etching his brow. "Rumors, the lies of violent drunks? A hundred scalped prisoners—soldiers like these—rotting in the Garden Valley sun?"

She remained silent, looking into his eyes.

"There's been savagery enough to go around," I said.

"A quiet girl, even skewered." He smiled. "But we fed you, so give us a dance, at least. A slow one if you need."

"For the war," the sandy-haired boy said from the shadows. "If you can call it that."

"Or the rain," another voice added. "It's been dry here for nearly a day."

"Many nights on the road," the doctor went on. "So little to look forward to. Give us a dance and then I'll free the boy of these arrows."

She turned to me, afraid.

"Please," I said. "Take them out now."

"If it's music you need, Collins is a bit of a singer, but I'm guessing you'll wish he hadn't." The doctor placed his hand heavily on my shoulder. His eyes held her like tongs.

"You'll take them out?" she asked, her voice high and sudden.

The doctor nodded. "Unskewering the skewered. It's my specialty." He gestured to the fire. "Really my only one. These boys can tell you. I run them out straight and true."

I tried to shrug off his hand, but a foolish hope kept me rooted in place. A dream of health and peace. Mercy watched me for a moment, my helplessness reflected in her eyes. Then she rose and stepped forward to the edge of the fire. Every eye followed her. Mosquitoes whined up from the riverbank. The trees behind her flung their black arms toward the dense ceiling of clouds. The dogs shifted from foot to foot.

A log popped in the flames. Mercy tossed away a picked-clean bone, and set one foot in front of the other. The soldiers leaned toward her. She began to dance. Straightening her back and drawing within herself, as if she might both grow and disappear. Stamping her feet in the dust, her dress flicking around her ankles, hips swaying, she tilted her head back and glided from side to side, finding the beat of a lost drum. Faster and faster, the arrow jumping and turning, as if she'd forgotten where she was, as if her body would leap up, join the column of flame, and vanish with the sparks.

I couldn't help but watch, transfixed.

A heavyset man in a buckskin vest stood and danced beside

her, his booted feet clumsy and slow in imitation, the leather fringe whipping around his waist. They twisted in the firelight, sparks rising between their faces. Grinning, the sandy-haired boy—my not-brother—rose also, and they passed her back and forth, the shaft of the arrow slipping between them, her limbs darting away from their hands.

"Don't touch her," I said.

The doctor's face was solemn in the glow. His thick fingers gripped my shoulder. "I was young once, too, and didn't understand," he said. "But these traitor girls, you have to break them. Like horses."

I tried to push him off, sluggish with whiskey, but his grip only tightened and another hand reached out to hold me.

More men danced into the firelight. Pinned, I could only see in flashes: Mercy's cheeks rigid in the orange heat, her arms clutching the thin dress around her chest. I wrenched my head to the side and bit down on the doctor's thumb, ripping flesh, trying to catch bone. He tore it free and a tremendous blow glanced across my mouth. Dizzy, bleeding, I fell back.

He leaned over me, spittle gleaming on his plump lips. "We've no shortage of bullets on this side," he hissed. "They don't come out."

The fire roared. More men stood. They pushed Mercy to her knees and circled around her. They forced her hands back from her chest. And I saw clearly how my life could end, though my body would carry on.

"Enough!" The innkeeper's voice rose above the shouts

and laughter. He stood behind the Browning, the barrel aimed into the circle of soldiers.

The doctor turned and released my shoulder. "Go to sleep, old man."

"They are guests here."

"She's no more a guest than one of your dogs."

The innkeeper shook his head. "They've paid, and I'll not see this on my land." His stomach strained against the buttons of his threadbare blue pajamas. A wisp of gray hair sprang from the open throat. "The next man to touch her joins the fire."

The doctor slowly rose. He stepped into the light. His face was cold and expressionless; his palm rested on the nickel-plated revolver at his waist. "What else do you have inside?" he asked. "What have you hidden away?"

The innkeeper spat onto the porch boards. He shifted the huge barrel to the doctor's chest. "You're not the first rooster to prance across my lawn. You nor your chicks." He looked around at the soldiers, then coughed, his whole chest shuddering. "I've seen far worse, and I'm not long for this world. I'd as soon leave this way as that."

The soldiers looked to their pistols and knives strewn at the edge of the circle. Then they looked at the long thread of ammunition trailing from the Browning's barrel. The doctor let his hand fall. He cursed softly.

Reluctantly, their faces hooded, the soldiers parted. Mercy pushed herself up. Her face was wet and bruised, her dress torn. She tried to run, and the heavyset man caught the arrow by the fletching. He twisted it, forcing her to sink into the pain, and whispered in her ear. Then he shoved her forward. She tripped, caught her feet, and ran, pitching forward through the dark toward the cabin.

I FOLLOWED, stumbling across the field and into the trees, through the door and through the dark room. Pausing only to pick up her knife, Mercy went out the open window into the night.

WE HID BENEATH the cabin's floorboards. On our sides, spaced by the arrows, our shoulders pressed between the dirt and the floor. I was too scared, too sick, to touch her. The doctor's blood, along with my own, seeped down my throat.

Saskatchewan. I'd drag him there by his tongue.

Mercy stared unblinking into the darkness. Her breath evened out. An immense and stubborn strength within her, like pillared rock in the center of a lake. The first time I'd seen her, in a hunting party with her brothers, she rode way out ahead of the men, her bow lofted, an arrow already nocked as her horse galloped beneath her.

I wished briefly that the stream of life could be reversed. That she could be unseen. And I, undone. For though I did not know what had happened to my family, I knew they had not escaped.

"We can run for the river," I whispered.

She didn't answer. Her eyes were fixed on the dark figures.

A raccoon carcass rotted behind my head. The stench made it hard to breathe. My jaw felt wired shut, my eyes wired open. I wanted to tunnel down into the earth and reemerge a fiery thing, huge and unfeeling. An angel of vengeance to purge the country's broken heart. Where two old lovers fought ceaselessly over something they'd killed long ago.

The soldiers drank and cursed until the fire died. Then one by one they unrolled sleeping mats or simply passed out where they sat. The innkeeper kept watch, his head lolling above the Browning, then jerking upright, until it, too, fell forward in sleep.

Mercy crawled out into the warm night. She held her torn dress together with her left hand, her knife in her right. She crouched for a moment, scanning the distant road, then took flight across the damp ground. Her limbs flickered between the tree shadows; her body bent forward at the waist. The arrowhead went ahead of her like the needle of some deranged compass. I followed as best I could, holding my breath and hobbling around the field.

The sleeping soldiers were mounds of blackness by the coals. Their weapons lay untouched in a ring. The doctor snored, mouth open, his lips a trembling socket in the center of his face.

Hazy light blanketed the horizon. The Dobermans rose when we crept behind the kennel. Mercy knelt at the gate. She took a pin from her hair and slipped it into the lock. Then she slotted her knife in as well and pressed her ear against the lock as she turned the pin. Her features drew together in concentration. Her eyes were black and depthless. Looking into them, I felt as if I were about to fall from the West.

The lock clicked and she pulled the gate open. We pressed ourselves behind it, using it as a shield as the Dobermans streamed out, their bodies ducking and gliding, a single, pulsing, silent gray mass charging the spit and the men. They knocked over what was left of the deer carcasses and fell on the soldiers. Jaws first: tearing, shaking, crazed by the meat and blood. The soldiers lashed out as they woke, pounding the sleek gray ribs. A shrieking growl was punctuated by screams. Locked together, man and dog rolled through the coals, black dust billowing around them.

We ran for the driveway, keeping to the shadows.

Shots tore open the night. The doctor shouted groggily and the uninjured soldiers scrambled back-to-back, firing indiscriminately into the mass of fur and limbs. The innkeeper leapt up, his eyes wild. He yelled for help and whistled to the dogs. Those still alive yelped, trying to crawl toward him. Coughing, choking, he called them by name. Then he turned the gun on the soldiers.

Birds burst from the treetops at the volley of gunfire, and the first ray of sun pierced the sky, as if the slaughter had broken wide the day.

Panting, Mercy stopped at the four-wheeler. Her knife was still open. She pointed the blade at my chest, silver and quick. Her eyes burned with a thousand-year hatred. The mountain reared up behind her, its ragged slopes outlined by purple dawn. I took the keys from my pocket, handed them to her, and climbed on the back.

"Kill me," I said. "But don't leave me here."

SHE DROVE EAST, the way we'd come, screams and gunfire fading behind us. The headlights made a pool of light up the dark mountain. The pain in my leg deepened on the bumpy road. I drifted in and out of consciousness, the warmth of her shoulder humming against my cheek. I dreamt of my mother, of being carried across a snow-dusted prairie at dusk.

When I woke, we were parked behind a shed at the pass. Mercy helped me from the four-wheeler. I staggered after her through the snow to the ski lodge. Then she doubled back, using a needle-covered branch to brush away our tracks. As I watched her bent figure, love and fear heaved inside me. I wanted to fall at her feet. I wanted to run from her, forever, to the cities I'd dreamt of on the coast.

Heart-strong, heart-weak.

The door hung loose on its hinges, the lock smashed, splinters on the floor. We climbed the stairs above the restaurant and looked down through the railing into the pillaged kitchen. Plate shards scattered the floor, the fridge lay on its side. A ketchup bottle had been thrown against the wall and the frozen red drops glistened like blood on the wood.

The attic was a small room in the roof's peak. Someone had slept there before: blankets and a tattered flannel shirt were mounded in the corner. Mercy found the seat of an old chair and helped me sit beside the lone window. She rolled one of the blankets under my leg to keep it raised, then she used her knife to saw the ends off the arrows in my thigh. She cut hers away, too, and tossed the fletchings into the corner. She held the arrowhead loosely in her left hand, as if she could not quite bring herself to give it up. Blood coated the obsidian.

"Constance lived for twelve years," she said, like a mantra. The rough stump looked alien above her hip.

"The soldiers will find us."

"They're dead."

"Your brothers."

"We've been punished enough."

Struggling, I lifted my head to the window. I looked out at the snow-covered trees, the snow-covered lift, and the snowy wash of an empty run. Even the sky was white. My leg felt lighter. The pain had faded and I had the feeling that if I didn't hold on to the chair, I might float away. That the earth and sky were only steps apart.

"I'm sorry," I said. "It's not what I thought it would be."

Somewhere out in space, a coyote howled—its long, high note speaking through time. Turning to a scream before yipping away to silence. Mercy lifted the arrowhead to the light. She held it for a moment, black tip glinting, then let it fall clattering to the floor. She lay down beside me and pulled the blankets over our shoulders. "We're alive," she said.

ACKNOWLEDGMENTS

THANKS TO MY TEACHER, DAVID FOSTER WALLACE, FOR HIS wisdom and kindness, which guide me to this day, Deborah Landau, Lydia Davis, Zadie Smith, and the rest of the faculty and staff of the MFA program at NYU, my friends, whose stories inspired this book, and most especially my parents, Candace and Doug, who've been the first to read my writing since I was five years old. Thanks to my agent, Chris Clemans, for his kindred spirit in guiding the manuscript to completion, my editor Tom Mayer, for lifting it higher, and the following organizations who supported me while I wrote: the Elizabeth George Foundation, the Jean Kennedy Smith Foundation, the Brush Creek Foundation, Writers Omi at Ledig House, Jen-

ACKNOWLEDGEMENTS

tel Arts, Caldera Arts Center, Ox-Bow, Mineral School, Vermont Studio Center, and Sitka Center for Art and Ecology.

The following stories have been previously published, some in slightly different form: "The Dancing Bear" in the *Minnesota Review*; "End Times" in *Narrative;* "Come Down to the Water" in the *Southern Review*; "Ways to Kill a Tree" in the *Chicago Tribune Printers Row*; "Stay Here" in *Ploughshares*; "Prey" in *Willow Springs*; "Too Much Love" in *Fiction*; and "Harvest" in *Hobart*.